JESSICA TANDY

They went looking for adventure,
And found themselves.

Camilla

with **ELIAS KOTEAS MAURY CHAYKIN GRAHAM GREENE**
... HUME CRONYN

MAJESTIC FILMS, NEWCOMM and MIRAMAX present a SHAFTESBURY-SKREBA production JESSICA TANDY BRIDGET FONDA in a DEEPA MEHTA film CAMILLA with ELIAS KOTEAS MAURY CHAYKIN GRAHAM GREENE and HUME CRONYN costumes MILENA CANONERO & ELISABETTA BERALDO editor BARRY FARRELL production designer SANDRA KYBARTAS director of photography GUY DUFAUX music by JOHN ALTMAN and DANIEL LANOIS executive producer JONATHAN BARKER screenplay PAUL QUARRINGTON based on a story by ALI JENNINGS producers CHRISTINA JENNINGS & SIMON RELPH director DEEPA MEHTA

MAJESTIC FILMS

Camilla

A Novel by
Christopher Davis

Based on the screenplay by
Paul Quarrington

Based on a Short Story by
Ali Jennings

WARNER BOOKS

A *Warner* Book

First published in Great Britain in 1994 by Warner Books

Copyright © 1993 by Camilla Films Inc. and
Skreba Creon-Camilla Films Limited.

The moral right of the author has been asserted.

*All characters in this publication are fictitious
and any resemblance to real persons, living or dead,
is purely coincidental.*

All rights reserved.
No part of this publication may be reproduced,
stored in a retrieval system, or transmitted, in any
form or by any means, without the prior
permission in writing of the publisher, nor be
otherwise circulated in any form of binding or
cover other than that in which it is published and
without a similar condition including this
condition being imposed on the subsequent purchaser.

A CIP catalogue record for this book
is available from the British Library.

ISBN 0 7515 1122 6

Typeset by Hewer Text Composition Services, Edinburgh
Printed and bound in Great Britain by Clays Ltd, St Ives plc

Warner Books
A Division of
Little, Brown and Company (UK)
Brettenham House
Lancaster Place
London WC2E 7EN

Chapter 1

The sea can often be whatever you want it to be. When you're happy, there is something about the play of light on the waves and the wash of sound that elevates happiness to a higher, cerebral plane. Even at night, the sound of the water accompanied by a faint glow of moonlight or starshine can be transcendent. And when you're unhappy, something about standing in the face of the sea washes that unhappiness away: your own little earthbound problems seem inconsequential in front of such grandeur.

Camilla had always looked to the ocean for answers or, at least, a little direction. All life began in water, and she thought that it somehow ended up there as well. It was a near-perfect day on the Georgia coast: sunny and not too windy or warm. As Camilla sat in her cast-iron beach chair looking out into the blueness, she wondered when her friends would make their appearance. Thin, eighty-something and dressed in a beige skirt with an

Oriental-looking jacket and a wide-brimmed sun hat, she scanned the horizon through a pair of antique opera glasses.

'Ma, there aren't any dolphins around here now.' Camilla's son, Harold, had broken the tranquillity of the moment, as usual, with his whining scepticism.

'Are you calling me a liar?' Camilla demanded.

'No, Ma. It's just hot out here in the sun.'

Harold preferred the sheltered world of the city to the wide-open reality of the great outdoors. A middle-aged film producer, he never ventured anywhere without his cellular phone. As he emptied sand from one of his expensive Italian shoes, Harold thought again about transferring his mother to a nursing home. He had thought about it often, but had not yet found the courage to do so, because he remembered well the fights they had when he sold the house in Toronto that he'd grown up in. And, given that his mother hadn't mellowed much, Harold knew that the fight over a nursing home would be worse, much worse.

Just then, Camilla, still staring through her opera glasses, pointed out at the ocean. 'You see,' she said.

Harold looked to where his mother was pointing, and there, maybe one hundred yards offshore, he could see the grey bodies of dolphins playing in the waves.

'I'll be damned,' said Harold, though Camilla didn't hear him. She watched the dolphins through her opera glasses and she was happy. No, more than happy, she was *alive*; she could feel the onshore breeze and hear the waves and see the dolphins frolic, and she felt at one with all of it.

A thousand miles away, in their Toronto apartment,

Freda and Vince were putting their vacation plans into action. Actually, it was Vince who had made the vacation plans – two weeks by the ocean in Georgia. Not your usual vacation spot, but Freda never liked to do things the conventional way. Freda was an artist, and at that moment, she was lost in a guitar track she was laying down on her tape recorder.

'Freda!' she heard from the outside. 'Freda!' She reluctantly shut off the tape recorder and after a moment's consideration, unplugged it, picked it up and headed out into the living room. She passed by Vince's drawing table and stopped to look at the drawing on it – an exquisitely detailed drawing of a bag of trash.

'Freda, are you coming, or what?' Vince yelled.

Freda put the tape recorder down, went to the window and hollered back, 'Be right down!' Then she stood, looking out for a moment. Vince was handsome and dark haired, and Freda smiled a little at the sight of him. After a last look around the apartment, she picked up her tape recorder and left.

Their car was an old Volkswagen Thing, a convertible. And, as Freda had often said, 'thing' was a good name for it, certainly much better than 'car'. It looked a little like a military-style, all-terrain vehicle, but much more flimsy, obviously built for neither comfort nor speed. Freda had often urged Vince to get rid of it, but for some reason Vince was fond of this rusting excuse for a car, and it was an argument that so far she had not managed to win. She hadn't given up hope, however.

Vince was impatient, and then he saw Freda come out with the tape recorder. 'Are you bringing *that*?' he asked.

'No,' said Freda sarcastically, 'I brought it all the way down here so it could wave bye-bye.'

'We don't have much room,' Vince said. Freda working was not what he had in mind for their vacation.

'What are you talking about?' said Freda, looking into the back seat and then starting to lift the recorder in.

'All right,' said Vince, reluctantly helping her move things around so that the tape recorder was secure. 'I just thought, you know, that we were on vacation.'

Freda shook her head. 'I brought some stuff,' she said. 'Just like you brought your paints. I thought that the general idea was that we're going to be Bohemian artists.'

Vince held up his hands in resignation. 'Let's just get on the road.' They climbed into the Thing, and Vince started it, put it in gear and pulled out into the street with a lurch.

They were not very comfortable together these days, which was part of the problems they were hoping a vacation would solve. And as Vince picked his way through the city streets, on to the highway and out of Toronto, they were each in their own worlds. Finally, when they were on the open road, the silence became too much, and Vince reached down and turned on the radio. The car filled with a quiet swell of strings and then the full orchestra came up suddenly, very loud. Vince reached down to change the station, just as a solo violin came in.

'Don't,' said Freda, catching his hand before he could turn the knob. Vince shrugged and turned his attention back to the road. Freda listened to the piece in silence as the miles passed, wondering what it was, wondering how she had missed knowing such a beautiful piece of music. The violin soared and sang and danced and rejoiced, and sometimes, when the entire orchestra joined in, it was almost painfully beautiful.

Vince found the music somewhat annoying, but something about Freda's intensity made him keep his thought to himself, and they travelled on to the beautiful sound of a violin concerto that Freda had never heard before. Sometimes a little fragment of melody would particularly appeal to her, and she would go over it in her mind to remember it for later use, or at least reference, and this made her think of composing. 'You know,' she said, the first words she'd uttered in more than thirty minutes, 'that machine I'm bringing?'

'Yeah?' Vince answered.

'Well, that's the same machine The Beatles used to make *Sergeant Pepper's*. Well, not the same machine. You know what I mean.'

'Yeah,' Vince said, 'but *they* were geniuses.'

Freda turned to look out the window.

'Not that you're not, or anything,' Vince hastened to add, 'but they were The Beatles.'

Freda didn't answer, and Vince said no more. The violin had just concluded a long, quiet movement and now was leaping and skipping and playing chords – something that Freda had not known was possible on the violin – with joyous abandon. It sounded terribly difficult and Freda searched through her bag for the little idea notebook she always carried so she could write down the name when the piece was finished. As she searched, the car slowed down and she looked up to see they had passed through Canadian customs and were slowing for the U.S. border guard, who was waiting outside her booth.

This was the guard's first posting, and she was young and eager – a farm girl who had got away from farm boys by joining INS. Although these people didn't look like terrorists, she thought, Can't be too careful these days.

'Where are you people from?' she asked officiously.

'Toronto,' Vince said.

'Ma'am?'

Freda nodded her head in agreement. 'Toronto.'

'Where are you going?' the guard asked, trying to deepen her voice.

'Georgia,' Vince said.

'Georgia,' Freda echoed.

'Holiday?'

'You bet,' Vince answered.

'And what do you people do for a living?'

'Bohemian artists, officer,' Freda said loudly, and Vince quickly interjected, 'Graphic arts.' The guard was a bit confused. She had some idea that graphic arts used graph paper or something, but she had no idea what 'Bohemian' meant.

'He's in graphic arts,' Freda said. 'I'm not in graphic arts.'

'And what do you do, ma'am?' the guard asked. She was beginning to think there was something kookie about these people, and she wondered whether she should call her supervisor.

'I'm a, a . . .' Freda thought for a moment. '. . . a composer.'

Vince smiled at the guard a little as if to say, humour her, and Freda saw it.

'Well I am!' she said.

'It makes it sound like you're Beethoven or something,' Vince said sarcastically.

'The woman asked me what I did!'

The guard decided that they were not terrorists, just another married couple – admittedly a strange married couple – having an argument, and besides, traffic was backing up, so she shrugged her shoulders and said, 'Move on through, please.'

'See, Freed?' Vince said with an I-told-you-so tone, 'I think what she really wants to know is how we make money, which is from my graphic arts company.'

'Move it out!' the guard ordered.

Vince put the Thing in gear and they lurched forward. 'What did you want me to say when someone asks me my occupation?' Freda asked. 'That I'm a leech? A parasitic growth on my husband's hairy back?'

'Hairy?' Vince said, with mock indignation.

Freda stared out the side window without answering, and suddenly she realized that there was piano music playing on the radio. 'Shit!' she said. 'I never did find out what that music was.'

'I was sick of it anyway,' Vince said, and he reached forward and twisted the knob until he found a sports channel broadcasting a baseball game. Freda just leaned back and tried to sleep.

Chapter 2

Johannes Brahms generally composed easily and fairly quickly, but this was not the case with his violin concerto. Brahms was not himself a violinist and probably would not have written a concerto for an instrument that he was not comfortable with if it had not been for his friendship with Joseph Joachim, one of the most famous violinists of the time. The concerto took some ten years or more in the planning and composition. Movements were included, then replaced. The entire piece was rethought and rewritten many times.

Finally, however, it was done: a muscular work in three movements. Brahms first sent it to Joachim for his comments, and Joachim wrote back that much of the music was playable on the violin and that some of it was actually enjoyable, which cannot have been the message that Brahms was hoping for. When Joachim later premiered the work, including a first-movement cadenza that he wrote himself, it did not receive immediate acceptance: for years it was called a 'concerto against the violin', and another virtuoso, Pablo de Sarasate, declared he would never play it.

In the early twentieth century, the Suzuki method of violin teaching, under which students start out playing simple melodies before learning to read music, had not yet been invented. So when the young girl Camilla began lessons with a stern German expatriate named Herr Professor Schoen – and he insisted on being referred to by both titles – it was done the hard way. This is not to imply that young Camilla was unhappy with strict lessons. Somehow, and no one was exactly sure why, she had started asking for a violin when she was three. Her parents thought the whim would pass. In fact, they hoped the whim would pass, because they had some idea – exactly how imperfect an idea they were to discover later – of what a small violin in the hands of a child would sound like for the first few years. Camilla continued to insist, however. For the next two years, whenever an occasion for gifts arose, she asked for a violin, and finally her parents gave in and Camilla's fifth birthday gift was a quarter-size violin. The next day she met Herr Professor Schoen for the first time.

Herr Professor Schoen was a large man with a round, red face and a heavy, drooping moustache. When his housekeeper showed Camilla and her mother into his studio for the first time, he asked Camilla's mother to leave and settled back into a huge brocade-covered chair. From there, he studied Camilla, who was standing nervously in the middle of the room, holding her violin case tightly with both hands in silence for a few minutes.

'Why do you want to play the violin?' he suddenly boomed.

'Because I do,' Camilla said quietly.

'That's not an answer, girl!'

There was silence in the room again.

'Well?' the Professor finally said.

'Because it's *beautiful*,' Camilla said. She pronounced the word very carefully.

The Professor smiled. 'It can be,' he said. 'It can be.'

He was to be her teacher for the next twelve years.

Chapter 3

It seemed to Freda that they had been driving almost forever, although it had only been a couple of days. Her back hurt, she felt filthy and she was tired. They finally reached Peabo, Georgia, on the third morning. And although they both tried, they could not figure out how to follow the real estate agent's directions from there to the house they were renting. Finally, although Vince insisted that he could find the place on his own, Freda got out of the car to ask for directions.

Peabo is a town that time has forgotten; it moves at a different, slower pace, where nothing is urgent, nothing really important except the weather and the presence of strangers. And there was more too, a kind of seediness that one writer described by saying that it seemed as if a carnival had just pulled out, as if the whole town was nursing a hangover and regretting some tawdry sexual encounter. Freda sensed some of this, but the only thing she noticed that was definite, identifiable, was that no one would look her directly in the face. When she asked directions from a couple of young men, one of them stared at his feet and the other seemed to be following the path of game birds flushed into the sky.

Freda did get accurate directions, however – which took them in exactly the opposite direction from the one that Vince had wanted to take. As they left the town, Freda noticed what seemed to be the local entertainment: a rather decrepit building with a large stuffed fish coming out of the roof and a sign that said, 'Fishin' Hole. Hoot Night Ever Friday'. Maybe I'll get Vince to go with me some night, Freda thought.

The locals had given them good directions and although there were several turns, they were never far from the sea and the fresh, salt air that breezed through the car. Smelling it, both Vince and Freda were happier than they had been anytime on their journey. 'This should be the driveway,' said Freda, as they came up to a long shaded drive that led to a house they could not see. Vince turned in.

'Unless the rental guy in Toronto lied, this is the place,' said Vince.

A grand old house with pointed gables and wide verandas came into view, and Freda said, 'Vince, it's magnificent!'

'Yeah it is,' Vince said. 'The only thing wrong with this magnificent house is we're not staying in it.' And he pointed off to the left to a small building that had once been a stable and then later was turned into a cottage for a caretaker. '*That's* where we're staying.'

'Well,' said Freda, 'it's semi-magnificent.'

'Sure. It's historical. We're staying in the servants' quarters.'

'Great! I'll be the maid and you be the lusty gardener.'

'Damn,' said Vince, 'I wanted to be the maid.'

They both laughed and for a moment, at least, the tension between them disappeared, and they got out of the car and walked towards the cottage hand-in-hand. Just as they reached the door, the Thing, which was parked on the slightest of inclines, started to roll backwards.

'Shit!' Vince yelled, and he ran to the car, pulled open the door and, with a mighty yank on the parking brake, the car came to a stop.

'I've told you that you should get that brake fixed,' Freda called.

Vince got out of the car and shook his head. 'I will,' he said, 'I will.' He reached in front of Freda and opened the door and held it open for her. The door opened on to a single large room that was almost the entire cottage. It was simply furnished with a few old chairs, a large wooden table, and a not-very-large bed near a window that looked out towards the big house.

'It's beautiful,' said Freda, and she meant it. It looked like just the kind of place where they could get their relationship back on track; the kind of place where she could compose; the kind of place where Vince would not be distracted by commercial stuff and might actually create some real art again.

'It's okay,' Vince agreed, as Freda ran and flung herself on to the bed and looked up at the exposed rafters. Vince followed. They lay together holding hands saying nothing, and then Freda took her hand away and placed it on Vince's chest and then played with a button on his shirt. Outside, they heard the sound of a large car on the gravel driveway and then the sound of two car doors opening and closing.

'Be careful with that, Harold,' they heard a woman's voice say.

'Ma,' a man's voice whined, 'ever since I'm a little boy, every time I go near this damned fiddle, you tell me to be careful with it. Did I ever even break one string on it?'

'It is not a fiddle,' the woman said imperiously.

'Maybe you and your violin would be happier in a nursing home,' the man replied, and then the voices were silent and a house door opened and closed.

Freda stroked Vince's chest for another minute or two. But the mood was broken. And finally Vince grabbed Freda's hand and held it still and said, 'So what side of the bed do you want?'

'Side? I want the whole bed!' said Freda, laughing and pushing Vince off.

Sleep came quickly that night, as fatigue from the journey took its toll of each of them. They slept in late the next morning so, when Freda awoke, she was both refreshed and ready to do something. Giving Vince a shake, she asked, 'How about a walk on the beach?'

'Maybe tonight,' Vince said. 'I'm still tired from the drive.'

Freda sat up and swung her legs off the bed. 'Come on, lazybones. You can go to bed early tonight if you want. We didn't drive all this way to stay inside.'

'Okay,' Vince said reluctantly. Freda threw on some tights and a short dress, and got a Walkman and a tape from a bag.

'Hey, I thought you wanted to commune with nature or something.'

'I thought you might listen to something I've been working on,' Freda replied.

'All right,' said Vince. The last thing he wanted to do was start an argument on the first real day of their vacation. Vince pulled on a pair of khaki pants and a T-shirt and followed Freda out the door.

They walked to the beach in silence. And when they reached the sand, Freda didn't turn on the Walkman. Instead, they just stood and looked at the beach fading into an opalescent haze in the distance and listened to the wash of the waves and the calling of birds. There were gulls and herons, and even the shrimp boats out on the water appeared to have wings, although it turned out to be nets protruding from the sides of the boats. The sea was calm, but the onshore breeze was strong enough to carry with it a fine mist of salt which remained when droplets of water, splashed up by breaking waves, evaporated in the sunlight. The mist smelled fresh and good and it stung a little.

They stood there a long while and then, without speaking, they turned at the same time and started walking towards the distant point where the beach and the water were indistinguishable, and Vince took Freda's hand and they walked in silence, happy and content. Finally, when they had walked for more than a mile, Vince said, 'I thought you wanted me to listen to some music.'

'You sure you want to?' Freda asked.

'I'm sure,' said Vince, and he gave Freda a kiss and she smiled and turned and handed Vince the earphones and turned on the Walkman. Again they walked without speaking, and when the piece was done, Vince handed Freda the headphones and said nothing.

'Well,' Freda asked. 'What do you think?'

'It's great.'

'You really think so?'

'Yeah, it's great,' Vince said. 'I have a little trouble with "parachute", but it's great.'

'Oh,' said Freda. 'You think it's great except for the central image.'

'It seems a bit unmusical, "parachute". I just think it's a little clunky, awkward. I mean "I'll always be your parachute, but you'll have to catch the wind." Shouldn't it rhyme or something?'

Freda didn't bother to answer. 'You know what this song needs?' she said. 'Horns. Brooding horns. Tubas and some tambourines. When we get back, I think I'll start a big band, with horns and maybe strings too.'

'Right,' said Vince.

'Do you think I could move on stage all right? You know, you gotta do some stuff when you're fronting a band, you can't just stand there.'

Both Vince and Freda knew that with Freda's fear of performing, she wouldn't be forming a band anytime in the near future, so Vince didn't directly answer the question. 'Hey,' he said, 'when I saw that band you were in, I never even noticed the lead singer. I only noticed you standing back there in the shadows playing that weird thing . . .'

'A flute? What's so weird about a flute?'

'. . . and I remember thinking, who is that beautiful girl?'

Freda laughed. 'Am I on *This Is Your Life*, or did you want sex or something?'

'Freda Lopez, this is your . . .' Vince stopped and held Freda so he was looking into her face. 'Did you mention sex?'

Freda didn't answer, but instead kissed him back, gently at first, then harder. And he pulled her tightly into him and they sank to their knees and then lay back, and things were progressing the way they have for centuries, when suddenly Freda pushed Vince's hand away from its target and said, 'We can't do this.'

'Why not? There's no one around.'

'We can't,' Freda insisted. 'We don't have a thing.'

Vince was exasperated. This was the closest they had felt together in months and Freda was worried about a condom. Why didn't she want children, anyway? 'What do you want me to do?' he said roughly. 'Run back to the house and get one?'

'You know I don't want to get pregnant,' Freda said, and she pushed Vince away and got up, brushed the sand off her clothes, and started walking back towards the house while Vince hurried to catch up.

'Why do you always walk so damned fast?' Vince asked.

'It's not my fault if you can't keep up,' Freda said, and she walked even faster. Vince stopped and watched her storm away and shook his head.

This time, the sea did not work its magic.

Freda was sitting outside in a chair listening to her Walkman and did not look up when Vince approached. 'Hey,' he said, 'what do you want for dinner?'

Freda turned the volume down, but didn't take the headphones off. 'Whatever,' she said.

'How about a barbeque?' Vince asked. 'I could drive into town and get some steaks and we could have seafood chowder or something.'

Vince liked to cook. And he spent a lot of time in Peabo, shopping for meals in the afternoons.

'Whatever,' Freda said again, and she turned the volume back up and looked away.

Within a few minutes, she was asleep and she never heard Vince leave and only woke up when he returned and rubbed her shoulder and said, 'Hey, Sleeping Beauty! How about some help?'

Freda shook her head, as if to clear it, and took off the headphones. The tape had long since run out, but Freda had been dreaming of music. She had been dreaming that she was at the front of a stage accepting clamorous applause for her performance of one of her songs. 'Okay,' she said. 'What are we having?'

'Steaks on the barbeque, some salad, and I bought some chowder that I'm going to jazz up a little.'

'I don't think I can eat steak,' said Freda.

'Huh?' This was something new.

'I'll just have the chowder and some salad,' she said.

'Whatever,' Vince answered, and they went into the cottage and unpacked groceries and put them away. Then, as Vince poured the chowder into a pan, he said, 'We should be thinking about children, you know. We should be thinking about more than just the two of us.'

'Why? I thought we were a couple.'

This was a conversation they'd had before; Freda

did not want children. Not now, when she hadn't done enough with her music; not now, when she hadn't yet attained her dream of becoming an established, respected singer-songwriter.

'We *are* a couple, Freed. We're just not a couple of college students. We can't spend our days doing Art with a capital "A" and our nights . . .'

'Vince, don't talk about art,' Freda interrupted.

Vince stopped stirring spices into the pot and turned around. 'Why shouldn't I talk about art? I'm an artist.'

'Right. A graphic artist.'

'The phrase is "graphic art", Freda, and I resent you saying it like it's graphic pornography.'

'Art and graphic art are not the same,' said Freda, echoing other comments she'd made over the past few months.

Vince was tired of this argument and he brought it home to Freda in a way that would hurt her the most. 'At least people see my work. You write all this music, and what's the point? No one ever hears it.'

'What do you mean?' Freda demanded. 'I make tapes all the ti— '

'Tapes are a substitute, Freed. Tapes are so you don't have to show up in person. Because you're afraid.'

'Oh yeah? Is that what you think?' Freda said, and she left the cottage, slamming the door on her way out, knowing that Vince was right. She stormed towards the beach and when she got there kicked furiously at the sand, muttering, 'I'll show him.' She remembered the club back in town and, as she picked up a shell and hurled it into the water, she decided she would try out her new song there. 'I'll show him,' she muttered again, and after a walk on the beach she made her way slowly back to the house and went inside and picked up her guitar while Vince was working at the kitchen counter. Neither of them said anything, and she went back outside and sat near the large barbeque that had obviously been built some years ago but made to last. Vince had already started a fire that was turning into glowing coals, and she played quietly, sometimes humming, sometimes singing a phrase, just at the edge of the fire's warmth.

From behind a curtain in the big house, Camilla watched.

Vince came out in a few minutes with a platter holding two Flintstone-sized steaks and put them on the rack over the coals. 'How would you like yours done?' he asked with false cheerfulness.

'I already told you,' said Freda, 'I don't want mine done.'

Jesus, Vince thought. 'These are really good steaks,' he said.

Freda put down her guitar. 'When I was growing up, the only friends I had were my father's cows. And it just occurred to me the other day that I have been devouring them.'

'Probably not the exact same cows,' Vince said, trying to make a joke.

But Freda was serious. 'Probably not,' she said, 'but how can I be sure? The safest thing is to just give it up.'

'Freda, you sure are a strange girl.' Vince shook his head.

They were so intent on their conversation that they didn't hear Camilla coming across the lawn, until she called, 'Is this true, Freda? Are you a strange girl?'

They turned and watched Camilla approach, walking almost like a queen approaching faithful subjects. When Camilla got closer she said, as if she hadn't known what they were doing, 'A barbeque! My goodness, I remember barbeques. You know, the Rajah of Lampur had the most magnificent barbeque. A pit was dug – it must have been twenty feet deep – and the animals, you see, were chased from the forest. Hundreds of animals.'

Vince looked at Freda and raised his eyebrows as if to say, Who *is* this lady? Freda shrugged. Camilla just continued on, regally, with her story. 'The animals were chased, they tumbled into the pit, and then the servants covered the pit with leaves and twigs and huge great logs of wood and the thing was set ablaze. It burned all the night long, and with the morning came the great feast.'

'Weren't there, you know, hairs and teeth and bones and stuff?' asked Vince indulgently.

'I would not know,' Camilla told him. 'I myself do not eat meat. I do not believe that the human body is capable of dealing with meat.'

'Mine is,' Vince said, and he prodded the steaks, creating a small flurry of smoke and flames, and causing Camilla to jump back.

'When you die,' she said sternly, 'there will be no less than six pounds of undigested red meat still in your system. Think about that, young man.'

'No kidding,' said Freda.

Vince shook his head. Eccentric old bat, he thought.

'And at the exact moment of death' – Camilla raised her index finger in the air – 'there is a sudden weight loss of six ounces. Scientists are unable to account for it. Some feel it is proof of the human spirit.'

This was getting a bit much for Vince. He wanted his steak, and he wanted to eat without the old lady around. 'Hold on,' he said. 'How do they know it's not just gas or something?'

'The gas has been accounted for,' Camilla said, speaking as if Vince was someone of limited intelligence.

Vince prodded the steaks again, and Freda mimed a look of disgust, which caused Camilla to smile, and then they heard a man's yelling from the direction of the big house. 'Ma! Ma! Where are you?'

'Oh no,' said Camilla. 'Here comes my son. Let us pay no attention to him. He is a buffoon.'

A man, a large man, came across the lawn waving an embarrassed wave from chest high. He was dressed in expensive clothing that just did not fit at all; various pieces were either too tight or too baggy or not tucked in. To put it succinctly, he looked like a slob.

'And a thief!' Camilla added, as Harold came up to the barbeque. Freda looked at her, puzzled.

'Ma,' Harold said again.

'Look, Harold. We're having a barbeque,' said Camilla.

'Ma, are you bothering these people?' Harold spoke as if Camilla were a child.

'I'm not bothering them,' Camilla said defensively.

'She's not bothering us,' said Freda.

Harold looked at the steaks on the grill and thought they looked mighty good. 'Ma, are you eating steak again? You know you shouldn't do that.'

'I am not eating steak.'

'She shouldn't eat meat, doctor's orders,' Harold said to the others. He looked again at the steaks sizzling on the grill, scenting the air. 'So, it's good you're using my barbeque. We don't use it much any more. You're Mr and Mrs Lopez, right? Harold Cara.'

Harold shook hands with Vince and Freda. 'I own these places.'

Vince wondered for a moment if there was a problem with them using Harold's barbeque. The real estate agent hadn't said how much of the grounds they could use. 'Would you like a steak?' Vince asked. He gestured towards the charring meat.

'Oh no, don't trouble yourself,' said Harold, looking at the steaks.

Vince thought that Harold looked like a good man with a knife and fork. 'It's no trouble at all,' he said, gesturing again towards the grill.

'Well, if you insist. Maybe just a small piece. Here, let me give you a hand.'

The two men did the manly thing with the grill and the meat. Camilla sat supervising silently, and Freda made seveeral trips to and from the cottage for utensils, food and beverages, until the men finally proclaimed the meat ready to eat and served themselves. The women filled plates with salads and grazed on their raw vegetables.

After dinner, Camilla led Vince to a pavilion overlooking the sea and waved her hand towards the water as if she owned it. For a few minutes, they just watched the late afternoon light play on the waves. 'So,' Camilla said suddenly, 'my son tells me you're Canadian. Is this true, Vincent?' She spoke as if she were interrogating someone of a lower order.

'Yes.' Vince just wanted to get away from this woman, but since she was, in a way, their landlady he felt he had to be polite.

'Is the city of Toronto still all abuzz about the performance I gave when I played the Brahms Violin Concerto,' Camilla leaned closer and lowered her voice conspiratorially, 'while my boobs threatened to pop out of a scandalously low-cut gown?'

What a nut case, Vince thought, trying to think of something to say. 'Camilla is sort of an unusual name isn't it?' he finally said.

'I was named for Camilla St Pierre. She was one of the greatest whores of all time.'

Vince could not think of an appropriate response.

Meanwhile, Freda and Harold were discussing film. Harold had told her that he was a commercially successful film-maker, but of 'art' films.

Freda could identify with that. 'I loved Peter Sellers in *Being There*,' she said.

'Oh, really?' said Harold. 'I found that rather pretentious.'

Taken a little aback by the comment, Freda asked, 'Would I have seen any films that *you've* made?'

Harold paused while he cut a large piece of roasted cow and chewed it vigorously and loudly. 'Well,' he said finally, 'for example, the last film I made deals with, um, a speculative view of the future as it pertains to human sexuality.'

Wow, Freda thought, a man who really does produce art. 'What's it called?' she asked.

'*Space Bunnies*,' Harold replied.

Freda greeted this with stunned silence.

As the sun began to set, the couples gradually drifted

together and carried on several non-intersecting conversations. The sun went down behind them, to the west, and the sea became darker and a twilight calm came over it. A cicada started, then died out. Everyone was quiet, tranquil. Camilla was now telling Freda the story of her career as a violinist. Freda was fascinated.

'All of high society turned out. I played the Brahms Violin Concerto. Do you know the Brahms, young woman?'

'Not really,' Freda said, but she decided that she would get a recording of it when they got back to Toronto.

'Everyone should know the Brahms.'

Meanwhile, Harold had been telling Vince about his business, and Vince smelled an opportunity. 'There's absolutely nothing wrong with low budget films,' Vince was saying, 'but it seems to me that when you try to scrimp at the marketing level, you're calling the films "cheap".'

I'll bet I can use this kid, Harold thought, and he said, 'These, to me, are statements fraught with good sense.'

The sun had set completely and an occasional firefly rose from the lawn. Camilla was still lecturing about the Brahms. '. . . and the technical aspects verge on impossibility,' she was saying. 'For years and years I practised, and finally my fingers tamed the notes. And then came the hard part: to make them sing.'

Freda was captivated. Camilla was everything Freda wanted to be: confident, successful, a real musician. 'How long did . . .'

'I think it's time to hit the hay,' Vince interrupted.

'Mrs Cara is in the middle of a story, Vince,' Freda said sharply.

'Oh, go on to bed, dear,' Camilla said, smiling. 'It doesn't matter. I'm always in the middle of a story.'

Harold offered to help clean up, but Vince and Freda declined. They all said goodnight and Harold and Camilla started across the lawn to the big house. Harold tried to take Camilla's arm, but she shook him off.

As soon as Freda and Vince got back inside, they began to argue about Camilla. And all the while they were doing dishes and cleaning the kitchen part of the room, they continued. Freda thought Camilla was wonderful, whereas Vince thought she was a nut. Finally, Vince grabbed a chair and set it in the middle of the floor. 'Look,' he said. 'This chair represents reality.' He picked up a newspaper and rolled it up. 'And this newspaper is the old lady. Now look, this is how far the old lady and reality are away from each other.' Vince backed away from the chair holding the newspaper in front of him, and when he reached the other side of the room, he abruptly turned and threw the newspaper out the open window.

Freda was disgusted, and she got ready for bed without speaking to Vince again. When she saw that he'd left a package of condoms on the bedside table, she huddled as close as she could to the edge of the bed.

Chapter 4

Herr Professor Schoen was a strict violin teacher. For the first year, the young Camilla spent as much time working with a paper and pencil as she did sawing away on the open strings of her little violin. First, she had to learn the lines and spaces of the stave. For the lines E–G–B–D–F, she had to memorize the little mnemonic, 'Every Good Boy Deserves Fudge', and for the spaces, FACE. Then she had to draw careful musical notes in the notebook that she was required to bring to every lesson. And, of course, there were also all of those different kinds of musical rests. Gradually, however, she put everything together, and when she could play a D Major scale she was assigned that little centuries-old tune known in English as *Twinkle, Twinkle Little Star*.

She practised for hours every day that week, bemusing her parents, who still thought that this fiddle thing was a little girl's fancy that would soon fade. However, when the day came for her lesson, she was so anxious that she was sick to her stomach in the morning and her parents said that she could skip her lesson that day. 'No!' she said firmly. And with much storm and drama she convinced her parents that she was well enough to go. When it came time for her lesson that afternoon, she still was not well – these days we'd say she was nervous, but back then her parents just thought she was 'high strung'. When she was ready and began to play, it was dreadful. Hardly a note was right, the bow wasn't tight enough, and her hands were shaking. It was about as bad a sound as a quarter-size violin can make. And a quarter-size violin can make some truly terrible sounds.

Herr Professor Schoen, surprisingly, was sympathetic. It wasn't known why he was teaching violin in Toronto instead of Berlin, or why he was teaching young people instead of touring the concert halls of the world. But there'd been some whispers about breakdowns and alcohol. Whatever the truth, Herr Professor Schoen understood nervousness. When Camilla finished the first time, he coaxed her through it again and again, singing along sometimes, other times making her laugh by comparing a note to some animal sound. And then, unexpectedly, she got it all right. That little quarter-size violin spun out as sweet and pure a version of *Twinkle, Twinkle Little Star* as any master could have done on a Stradivarius, and tears came to Herr Professor Schoen's eyes. As her last note faded, he sat at the piano and began a little introduction and then nodded to Camilla when it was time to come in and she played it again, as beautifully as before, accompanied by delicate arabesques on the piano. It was the first time that Camilla truly made music, an experience that many people are not fortunate enough to have in their entire lifetime. It was to influence the rest of her life.

Chapter 5

Vince liked to sleep late, until the early afternoon. When he finally did get up, he found a note from Freda saying she'd gone for a long walk on the beach and that if Vince felt like it he could get some things they needed in town. A list was printed at the bottom on the note. So much for togetherness, Vince thought, though he did notice that Freda had left her Walkman on the table beside the note. She probably forgot it, he thought. He didn't particularly like being in the strange cottage alone, so he dressed and left quickly for town.

Freda got back to the cottage only a few minutes after Vince left; she had actually gotten a couple of miles down the beach and then turned and hurried back, thinking that she'd been a little tough on Vince and thinking she could still catch him in bed and perhaps they could have sex and make up a little. When she saw that the Thing was gone from the drive, she was sad that she'd missed him and was about to go in to get her guitar and work on her new song when she heard the sound of a violin coming from the big house. It was a wandering, formless melody, nothing that Freda recognized, but still captivating, and Freda turned and walked towards the house. When Freda reached the porch she hesitated, then tiptoed up the steps and across the porch to a window, where she tried to peer through a gap in the curtains. Suddenly the music stopped, the curtains flew apart and Camilla's face appeared. Freda jumped back and the curtains closed. At first Freda was embarrassed, but then, in an effort to save face, she went to the front door and rapped on it loudly. There was no response, so after a minute or two she did it again, and then the door flew open.

'Yes? What do you want?' Camilla demanded.

'I heard some music,' Freda said hesitantly.

'Well, come in, girl, come in,' Camilla said, and she turned and marched back into the house and Freda followed, shutting the door behind her.

The house was dark and gloomy, with faded wallpaper and heavy wooden furnishings. The curtains were all drawn and it took Freda's eyes a moment or two to adjust to the light. First she saw a portrait of Camilla that looked as if it had been painted by Modigliani. Then she noticed an old, yellowed framed poster in a place of honour on the wall, walked to it and read it aloud. 'Camilla Cara at the Winter Garden. May first.' Freda looked at the poster even more closely. 'Hey,' she added, 'that's in Toronto.'

'Yes,' Camilla said grandly. 'I stepped on to the stage. There was absolute silence. I drew a deep breath, placed the bow on the strings and then abandoned myself to the muse. I came to, somewhere in the midst of a twelve-minute standing ovation.'

'You know, they opened that place again. The Winter Garden, I mean. It's all fixed up just like it was. It's really nice.'

Camilla continued as if she'd not been interrupted. 'I have heard that a young man committed suicide after that concert, his heart destroyed by the unspeakable beauty, but I do not know that for certain. People are so prone to exaggeration.'

While Camilla was telling Freda the story of that concert, practically note by note, Vince was finishing his shopping. He had even, to his surprise, managed to find a copy of the *Toronto Star*. What he did not know was that the news vendor carried a few copies of the paper just so that Camilla could walk in and buy one if she wanted. The store owner really didn't care if he sold any or not, because Harold paid for five copies a day just so he wouldn't have to hear his mother complain that they were too far from civilization.

As Vince walked by a local saloon with his groceries, Harold saw him from inside and hurried out, his beer still in his hand. 'Lopez!' he called.

Vince stopped. 'Oh, hi,' he said.

'I'm having a beer. You want a beer?'

'I don't think so,' said Vince.

'Come on,' said Harold. 'This is a great place – the Pirates' Den, so called because the people who live around here are under the erroneous impression that the coast was visited by buccaneers.'

'Maybe some other time.'

'Hey,' said Harold, 'carpe diem.' He pronounced

'carpe' without the e, so it sounded like the name of the fish. 'Carpe diem!'

Vince was puzzled for a moment, and then he said, 'Oh yeah, that was in that movie, that Robin Williams movie, the *Dead* something.'

'What movie?' Harold roared. 'It's Latin. It means seize the day by the goddamn balls. It means have a beer with Harold.'

'I really should hurry home,' said Vince.

'Never hurry anywhere! Come on, I'm buying. I'm a fucking millionaire!'

'Well, maybe one quick one,' said Vince. 'But I'm buying.'

'Fine, you're buying,' Harold agreed. 'But I want to talk some business with you, young man.'

An hour later, Vince and Harold had had several beers, and Harold had offered Vince a job. While this was happening, Freda and Camilla were drinking lemonade in Camilla's kitchen, and Freda was telling Camilla about her own career dreams, which were becoming more elaborate by the minute.

'I was thinking of putting together a band,' she said. 'You know, horns, strings, back-up singers, the whole deal, so that I could be the front man. You know, do some of those moves.'

Camilla had no idea what moves Freda was talking about, but she listened politely.

'. . . but then I thought, no, touring can be such a drag. Performing is such a major pain in the butt.'

Camilla would not let anyone say anything bad about performing. 'But there is no feeling that approaches it,' she said, raising her finger. 'The audience stares at you, silent and expectant.' She was silent for a moment. 'You draw out a single note.' More silence. 'You give life to sprites and goblins.'

What a weird thing to say, Freda thought. 'But don't you get, you know, frightened?' she asked.

'I,' Camilla said grandly, 'am the great Camilla. They are peasants.'

'I wish I had your attitude,' said Freda.

'Help yourself,' said Camilla. 'I shall show you the music room. It was once Ivor's writing room. But Ivor died.' Camilla stood and motioned expansively for Freda to follow her.

'Who was Ivor?' Freda asked.

'My husband,' said Camilla. 'Harold's sire,' she added, as if talking about some disgusting mating that she'd had nothing to do with.

Freda definitely got the impression that Camilla had not been fond of her husband. 'He was a writer?' she asked.

'Oh yes,' Camilla said as she threw open a door. 'He was a famous novelist.'

The room was dark and dusty. It didn't look as if it was used very often. Camilla opened some curtains and in the light everything look dingy. The room was filled with old musical instruments. A wooden music stand stood in a corner. Place of pride was taken by an enormous grand piano.

'Come,' said Camilla, leading Freda towards a floor-to-ceiling bookcase filled with books and a few framed photos of a man with a boy. 'Ivor's oeuvre,' said Camilla. 'Here's one: *Under the Yellow Sun*.' She handed a book to Freda, who opened it and started reading a page at random.

'It's about a missionary in China who falls in love

with a nurse,' said Camilla. 'They have a child out of wedlock. A Chinese warlord steals the baby and raises him as his own.'

'Sounds good,' Freda said, politely.

'It's a piece of dung,' Camilla told her. She took the book back and replaced it. 'He also wrote extensively on the subject of hothouse flowers. Here's *Orchids by Indirect Sunlight*,' said Camilla, leafing through another volume. 'A bit dry.'

While Camilla seemed momentarily engrossed, Freda turned to the thing in the room she was really interested in: the grand piano. It was as old as everything else in the room, but it looked as if it hadn't been used very often over the years. Freda wondered if the instrument was in tune, and she reached out and gingerly played a single note.

'Never show weakness in front of a musical contraption, girl!' Camilla ordered, making Freda jump and pull her hand back.

'I'm not very good,' Freda said. 'I've never taken lessons or anything. I just play . . .'

'You're taking a lesson now,' Camilla said. 'Sit down.'

Freda sat on the bench tentatively.

'Settle in,' Camilla ordered. 'Get comfortable.'

Freda pulled the bench a bit closer to the keyboard and got as comfortable as she could with this strange woman ordering her around.

'Good,' Camilla said. 'Now play something.'

'I . . .'

'Just play something! Have a bash at it.'

Freda put one hand out and played a chord very quietly. The notes did not all sound at the same time, so it was partly like a chord and partly like a small arpeggio.

'We must work on that,' Camilla said. 'You want all the notes to sound at the same time. Now let's have a little authority.'

The two women spent more than an hour at the piano, and at the end of that time Freda could play a solid progression of chords from one of her songs. She was also tired, and she finally said she could not absorb anything else.

'Fine, girl,' Camilla told her. 'We will resume tomorrow.'

The two women chatted for a few more minutes, but Camilla seemed tired. And Freda, experiencing the same feelings that so many musicians have felt after an inspiring lesson, wanted to practise. So she said goodbye and within five minutes was back in the cottage with her guitar in her arms playing the song she'd been working on. She was playing much more assertively than she had in the past and she realized it, which was even more inspiring. She heard Vince drive up, but didn't stop; she didn't even stop when he came in.

'I've got to talk to you,' said Vince.

'Talk,' Freda told him, not stopping playing.

'Can you put that down for a minute?' asked Vince. 'Please.'

'I can hear you,' Freda told him. She continued to play.

Vince knew that Freda was going to be unhappy at what he had to say, so he didn't push the point about the guitar. 'After what I've told you what I'm going to tell you, I want you to pause. Pause and reflect. Okay?'

'Okay,' said Freda after a pause. She didn't think Vince's news was going to be good.

'Harold's offered me a try-out. Film posters. I get to plan the whole campaign.'

Freda stopped playing the guitar. There was a long silence. 'Yeah?' she finally said.

'Yeah!' Vince threw a suitcase on the bed and started packing clothes into it, throwing in the box of condoms from beside the bed in the process. 'Why aren't you getting ready?' he said when he saw that Freda hadn't moved.

'Getting ready? For what?'

'Leaving for Toronto,' said Vince. 'Look, life isn't a holiday. When opportunity knocks, you answer the door.'

'You sound like a business seminar. What happened to you, anyway?' Freda was very disappointed, more disappointed than she could even express. This was supposed to be the time when they rediscovered their artistic passion, and now Vince was going to do posters for porn movies. And just for the money. What difference did money make, anyway? They'd always had enough to eat, always had a decent place to live.

'You tell me, Freed. What happened?'

'Don't you remember? You'd paint me playing the guitar naked. I'd sit, playing the guitar naked, and write a song about you painting me. Remember those times?'

Freda stopped. They'd been the happiest times of her life. The two of them had been so in love that nothing could come between them. 'I just had an idea,' Freda said, after a minute or two of silence during which Vince continued to pack. 'I'm staying.'

'Here? By yourself?'

'Some people live their whole lives by themselves. I think I can manage a couple of weeks.'

Vince was in no mood to argue. This was his big opportunity and Freda didn't care; hell, she didn't even see it as an opportunity. 'What are you going to do here by yourself?' he asked.

'Work on my music. Compose,' she said. Spend some time with Camilla, she thought, but didn't say.

Vince had had it with this pseudo-composing business. 'Freda, look. I don't want to hurt you, but do you know what your music is? It's your hobby. And you don't need to be here to do it. You can have your hobby anywhere. I, on the other hand, have a new job, something I can get excited about, and I have to go back to Toronto.'

Few words could have been crueller, and when Freda spoke, it was very quietly. 'Okay,' she said. 'Fine.'

'You're coming with me,' Vince said. It was an order, not a question.

'Why?' Freda asked.

'Because that's the way it works.'

'It doesn't work,' Freda shouted suddenly.

There was nothing that Vince could do or say over the next half hour that could change Freda's mind, and he tried everything: threats, bribes, kindness, tearful apologies. All she would say was that they both had things to work out, and that she liked the sea and wanted to stay close to it for as long as possible. Finally, Harold was outside tooting, and Vince had to go.

'You sure you won't come?' he said once again, and Freda answered by playing her guitar. She did allow herself to be kissed on the cheek, but she didn't

[38]

respond, and she didn't come outside when Vince finally got into Harold's Cadillac.

'She's not coming,' Vince told Harold.

'Really?' said Harold. He was surprised, but he didn't care.

'Really,' Vince said. 'I'll leave her the car and come with you to the airport.'

'I'm glad she's staying,' Harold then said. 'She can keep an eye on my mother.'

'Sure,' Vince replied. He didn't want Harold to know how truly upset he was; even Freda had thought he was not concerned about her, but he was, and he did love her although he was not very good at showing it anymore.

'My mother is not exactly Miss Cogency, you know,' Harold said, and Vince nodded.

Over the next week Freda had more time to herself than she'd had for years, and during that time the sea worked its magic. Sometimes she awoke early, while it was still dark, and watched as the sun rose beyond the horizon, out over the sea. During these early-morning times, Freda had few thoughts at all except an appreciation of the extraordinary beauty she was privileged to see. Later, however, at midday, when she walked along the beach and let its sound wash over her, she was often not aware of its beauty at all. Instead, she heard songs in her head. She heard lyrics and chord progressions and instrumental solos. And in those midday times, she composed better than she ever had, tapping into reservoirs of talent she never knew she had. The phone rang a lot those days, and at first it required a real effort for Freda to ignore it. But eventually she barely heard it through the songs in her head. Even though she assumed it was Vince, it no longer seemed important.

Not only did the sea work its magic; Camilla began to work magic too. She gave Freda the beginnings of a self-confidence she'd never had. That Friday, Freda took her guitar, got into the Thing and drove to the Fishin' Hole. It was 'Hoot Night' – open mike, where anyone with nerve can get up and perform – and the place was packed. She found herself a seat at an empty table way at the back and listened to the entertainment for a while. It was not very good: loud singers and out-of-tune guitars alternated with would-be stand-up comics telling well-worn or off-colour jokes – or both. Freda was ready to bolt when a waitress came over to the table. 'What'll it be, hon?' the waitress asked.

Freda really wanted to leave, but then she thought of Camilla and Camilla's strength and she pointed to her guitar case on the floor and said, 'Just water, please.'

'Mitchell!' the waitress called. 'You've got another lamb for the sacrifice!' She held her hand high in the air and pointed down at Freda's head. 'Everybody has to order a drink, hon,' she told Freda. 'House rules.'

'Ah . . .' Freda thought for a moment. She did not drink much alcohol and did not know a lot about cocktails. 'I'll have a Bloody Mary without the alcohol.'

'Same price with or without,' the waitress said.

'That's okay.'

'One bloody shame!' the waitress yelled at the bartender, causing Freda to jump. She wished she were back at the cottage. In fact, for the first time since she'd been in Georgia, she wished she were back in Toronto. The drink arrived just as a man took the microphone and introduced someone named Eddie Edsel, who immediately began abusing his guitar. Freda winced, but the crowd seemed to know Eddie and were very appreciative.

Freda had already decided that she should leave when the man who introduced Mr Edsel came to the table. 'Hi,' he said. 'I'm Mitchell. I own the joint. Pretty neat, huh?'

Freda nodded.

'So, are you going to play your guitar for us?'

'Maybe,' Freda said tentatively.

'Great. Let me write down your name. I write down all the names on these little cards and mix them up, then that's the order. What's your name?'

Freda was quiet.

'Hey, it's not a trick question. What's your name?'

'Ah, Freda. Lopez, I suppose.'

Mitchell wondered why Freda was having trouble with her own name, but he didn't comment on it. Instead, he said, 'What a great name. Sounds like Zorro's girlfriend, or something.'

'Ah, right,' said Freda.

'Okay,' said Mitchell. He patted her shoulder. 'Good luck.'

I'll need it, thought Freda.

Mr Edsel finished his set and Mitchell took the mike. 'That was Eddie Edsel.' There was a lot of applause. 'And – surprise, surprise – he wrote that song himself. No kidding.' Mitchell looked down at the cards in his hand. 'And now we have a real treat. Someone who's never been here before. Ladies and gentlemen, please welcome Zorro's girlfriend, Freda Lopez!'

There was a little applause as Freda walked up from the back, but it had stopped by the time she reached the stage and didn't start again. Freda stood well back from the mike, too far back to be heard well. 'Hi, good evening. I'd like to play a new song that I just finished yesterday.' Someone laughed. 'I've practised it,' Freda said, and she began to play, and when the verse came in she sang very quietly.

'Louder!' someone shouted, and Freda sang a little louder and her voice cracked. There was more laughter, but she went on. It was a dismal, disheartening performance. The audience, mostly men, became increasingly inattentive, holding inter-table conversations, laughing, flirting with the waitress, and suggesting to each other things that Freda might be better at than singing. When she was finally finished, there was almost no applause, although someone did shout, 'Get the hook!'

Freda wanted to talk to Vince, and she wanted to talk to him right then. She didn't want to wait until she got back to the cottage. The only public phone was by the back of the bar, and it was already in use by Mr Edsel, who was obviously talking to his girlfriend.

'Veronica,' he was saying, 'I floored them. The next step for me, career-wise, is like the moon!' Freda sat at the end of the bar trying not to cry. The bartender said nothing, but put a Bloody Mary – this one with a little vodka in it – on the bar in front of her. She didn't touch it, and as soon as the next performer was under way, Mitchell came over and stood beside her. 'It was good, really,' Mitchell said.

'I was awful,' said Freda simply.

'No, really, Freda Lopez, it was good. It was a nice song. These people, though, they're like a pack of wolves, you know.'

Freda nodded in agreement.

'I mean,' Mitchell went on, 'if they sense fear, you're a dead duck. A very feral crowd, man. You just got to get some, you know, self-confidence.'

'The story of my life,' said Freda sadly.

'It was a good tune, though, man. Really. Very poetic.' Mitchell patted her on the shoulder and wandered off. By then, Mr Edsel finished on the phone.

It took Freda several minutes to complete the call, because she insisted on paying for it herself with change and not calling collect. Finally, Vince answered. Freda could hear *The Singing Chef* in the background on Vince's television, and she was silent for a moment while Vince said, 'Hello. Hello? Hello!'

'Hi, Vince,' said Freda very quietly.

'Freda? Freda! Where have you been all week?'

'Here.'

'Where's "here"? What's all that strange noise in the background?'

'That's music, Vince.' Already Freda realized that the call was not going to be what she'd hoped.

'You're at that place? You've been hanging around that bar place?' It was as much an accusation as a question.

'I've been at the house,' Freda said strongly.

'No, you haven't. I call all the time and the phone just rings and rings.'

'I don't always answer.'

'Never answer, is more like it,' said Vince. 'Too busy composing?' he asked sarcastically.

'Yes.' Freda wanted to hang up.

'I bet even Beethoven would occasionally answer the telephone. And before you say anything, that was a joke.'

'Very amusing,' said Freda.

'So when are you coming home?'

Freda had wanted to talk to him about her failed performance, but it was obvious that Vince was not interested. 'Let's start again,' she said. 'Hello, Vince?'

'When?' Vince insisted.

'No, it's me, Freda.'

'What?'

'That was a joke.'

'No, it wasn't, Freda. That was *avoidance*.'

'No,' Freda said very loudly. '*This* is avoidance!' She slammed down the receiver, grabbed her guitar, and ran out as someone on the stage was telling a joke about 'fairies' – and not the tiny mythical creatures with wings.

Freda wasn't depressed on the drive home; she was angry. When was Vince ever going to take her seriously? She'd been composing, and had been working well, and Vince treated it as though it was some amusing – and to him annoying – little hobby.

Not conscious of the drive home, she found herself at the driveway and turned in with a squeal of tyres and accelerated past the big house towards the cottage. Then, she stopped and backed up, accelerating as she did, and slammed on the brakes, remembered the parking brake, gave it a vicious yank, and jumped out. She stood for a moment on the driveway, listening. Cicadas called in the trees, and from inside the house came strange sounds: a violin, but swooping and sliding in almost otherworldly music.

Freda listened for a moment, and she thought it sounded like whales. She was right. Camilla was watching a nature show on TV, which that evening was about humpback whales, and, in her nightgown, she was playing a responsive counterpoint to their recorded songs. Although the timbre of the violin was different from that of the whales' songs, Camilla's improvised composition fit perfectly. She concentrated hard, with her eyes shut so she could hear the tones better. And when Freda first knocked on the door, Camilla ignored it. After a minute, another knock came, and Camilla continued to play for another minute or two before going to answer it. She opened the door just as Freda was going back down the steps.

'Come in, girl!' Camilla said.

Freda turned back. 'I know it's late, and I don't want to bother you. You probably want to go to bed or something.'

'I've been to bed! Come in! You know how much sleep I seem to require these days? Approximately eighteen minutes a night. Come in.' Camilla went back into the house, leaving the door open, and after a moment Freda followed her down the hall to the kitchen in the back of the house.

Camilla said nothing, so Freda began to talk, nervously and all at once. 'So what have you been up to tonight? You know what I did, I went down to that place, that hoot club. Things didn't go at all well.'

Camilla sensed there was a problem. 'Let us drink liquor,' she said firmly. 'I think I have some sherry.' She took a half-full bottle of sherry from behind the sink, leading Freda to think that she probably took 'liquor' more often than she wanted anyone to know.

Camilla got two teacups from a cupboard and said, 'I've been partial to sherry ever since the Duke of Nottingham used it as a tool of seduction. The ensuing experience put me right off Dukes, but I am fond of this stuff.' She raised her cup in a salute and then drank off a good portion of its contents.

Freda raised her cup and did the same. 'It's good,' she agreed.

The women were silent. Camilla obviously did not want to talk about Freda's unfortunate performance experience, and Freda was content to let the silence unfold, like a flower unfolds in the imagination. Finally, Freda did speak, and it was a contemplative monologue, not needing or desiring a response.

'I'll tell you one thing, people don't want music. They just want entertainment. And you've got to ask yourself, do you want to be an entertainer? You don't really need to play in front of people, and the worst thing is, if you're not perfect, if you don't get it right, they turn on you.'

Something Freda said seemed to upset Camilla, and she got up abruptly without speaking and walked out of the room. After a minute or two, Freda followed. Camilla was standing on the veranda in the dark, surrounded by the sound of nearby insects and the distant surf. Neither of the women said anything for a while. Finally, it was Camilla who spoke first.

'I was lying to you, dear.'

'Huh?' Freda was still thinking about her performance.

'About that famous concert,' Camilla said, as though Freda would of course know what she was referring to. She went on without a pause. '. . . by implying that the glory sprang solely from my genius. I did, of course, play upon the most beautiful handmade instrument. A violin made especially for me.'

Then Freda remembered something she had clipped from a *Toronto Star* that Vince had bought in town. 'Hey, you won't believe this,' she said. She took a newspaper clipping from her back pocket, unfolded it, and read aloud: 'The Brahms Violin Concerto.'

Camilla was still in the past. 'The Brahms. The exquisite, the transcendent. My greatest triumph.'

'This is the unbelievable part,' Freda said. 'You know where it is?'

'I was supposed to meet my lover after that concert,' said Camilla, remembering, reliving, 'but something went dreadfully wrong.' She fell silent a moment. 'I never saw him again.'

After another moment's pause, Camilla snapped back to the present. 'What were you saying, dear?'

'The Winter Garden,' Freda continued. 'The newly refurbished Winter Garden Theatre. In Toronto.'

Camilla smiled. 'That's right, dear.'

'No! That's where the concert is. That's where they're having it.' She held the clipping in front of Camilla's face.

'Oh.' Camilla was confused for a moment, but she recovered. 'We should go.'

'Well,' Freda said thoughtfully, then more aggressively, 'let's.'

'Let's what, dear?'

'Let's go to the concert. Me and you.'

Camilla was suddenly unsure of herself; she wasn't comfortable with the idea of actually taking action. 'I'm not sure that Harold will let me,' she said timidly.

'Well, you know, screw Harold!'

'Oh, absolutely,' Camilla said. 'He's a swindler.'

[47]

Then she had another concern. 'But who would look after my plants?'

'I guess it was a stupid idea,' Freda said reluctantly. 'I just thought it might, you know, work out. I can go back and turn myself in, and you can hear the Brahms again.'

Camilla seemed lost in thought again. After a minute, she asked, 'Do you think we could go to Niagara Falls?'

Freda thought it was a weird question, but she said, 'I don't see why not. It's on the way.'

Camilla was off somewhere again. 'I love waterfalls. I've seen them all. The Victoria Falls, the mighty Peruvian Quillabamba. But one of the ironies is that I've never . . .' Suddenly, she was in charge again. 'I've reconsidered. I shall indeed take you to hear the Brahms.'

'Great,' Freda said. 'All right!'

'Bottoms up,' Camilla replied, and she emptied her cup in one swallow.

Chapter 6

In the same time zone, but a thousand miles away, a man sitting at a bench was working on a violin. The room was cluttered with pieces of violins in progress, keeping company with pieces of disassembled violins that needed repair. There were pieces of wood ranging from tiny blocks to large, thin sheets. And everywhere there were the tools necessary to work with wood: chisels, mallets, coping saws, both tiny and large, planes, blocks with sandpaper tacked on them, two-handled draw shaves, and 'C' clamps in all sizes. If the craftsman used power tools, there was no evidence of it. In another section of the workroom were the expensive varnishes and soft brushes that would finish the work, and nearby several pieces of instruments were drying.

The man's hands revealed his age. They were thick-veined and gnarled, covered with the spots of old age; they moved with difficulty, but lovingly and still expertly. They picked up a new thin rectangle of wood and, after feeling the grain from different directions, carefully drew in the shape of a violin, without using a stencil, and the shape was true and graceful. When the front was cut, it would be used as the pattern for the back. This was to be a new instrument, built for the pleasure of it, not for a commission. When the outline was finished, the hands picked up a thin-bladed coping saw and carefully began to cut.

Years earlier, when Camilla was still young, not even ten, the violin maker had first gotten his love of the instrument from her. Actually, his love was not for the instrument, but for the girl he saw pass by his father's cabinet-making shop once a week, carrying her tiny violin. She was always beautifully dressed and always walked a few deliberate steps in front of her mother. For months, the boy hoped for an opportunity to talk to the girl. But when the first encounter happened it could hardly have gone worse. The girl and her mother actually came into the shop late one afternoon after a lesson. And while the mother was discussing the repair of a sideboard, the boy – Ewald Heinrich by name – stood and stared without speaking. Finally, when Camilla and her mother were leaving he blurted out, 'Is that a fiddle?' and Camilla answered frostily, 'No, stupid, it is a violin.' She left without looking back, and the young Ewald was crushed as only a boy can be.

The next day he asked his father to show him how to make a violin, and his father, as unaware of what the motivation was as only a father could be, chuckled indulgently and told Ewald, 'Perhaps someday.' It was, however, the first time Ewald had showed any interest at all in his father's art. And, two weeks later, after

Ewald was sure that his father had forgotten, a large book arrived at the shop, a book with designs for violins, with drawings of each piece and explanations of how the pieces fit together; there was a separate section on varnishes and finishing. That afternoon, Ewald started building his first instrument.

Chapter 7

Freda packed for their journey slowly, knowing that it was the beginning of the end of her liberation. She would go home to Toronto, resume life with Vince and, she knew, things would be much the same as before or even a little worse. Her return would be seen by Vince as a capitulation, an admission that her musical career was going nowhere. And she knew – and for the first time admitted to herself – that that was at least partially true.

If the trip to Toronto was an act of contrition for Freda, for Camilla it was pure defiance. When Freda had almost finished packing the car, Camilla emerged from the big house with a small, faded carpet bag and her violin case. Freda thought that the carpet bag was peculiar luggage for someone who had done so much travelling. But before she could say anything, Camilla said, 'Ready, girl?' and handed her bag to Freda. She clung to the violin case herself, however, and climbed into the Thing. After Freda stowed the bag in the back and got into the front, Camilla commented, 'This certainly is an odd vehicle.'

'It's Vince's pet,' said Freda.

'Well, never mind,' Camilla said. 'Drive! We are off to hear the Brahms.'

As they drove down the street towards town, Camilla turned back and looked at the house and then muttered, 'Good riddance.'

Freda signalled a turn that would have brought them on to the mainland and, eventually, on to the big interstate. 'No,' Camilla said, 'we will follow the water,' and she directed Freda to turn off on to a little road that didn't look as though it was going to lead anywhere important.

'Are you sure you know where we're going?' Freda asked.

Camilla said, 'Of course, girl.' Then, abruptly, a few seconds later, 'Turn there!'

The new road turned and ran along the water. Pelicans sat on posts, occasionally troubling themselves to rise into the air, take an awkward headfirst cannonball into the water, and then return to their perch with whatever goody they had captured. And there were shrimp boats everywhere, either returning to port or heading out in search of their bounty from the sea. The drive was pleasant, and the women watched the landscape, the pelicans and the workboats in silence. At one point, Camilla directed Freda across a causeway. Although the area had had its splendours, they were long gone. Now it was a place where people lived to make a living from the sea. Almost everything had a tired, rundown look. Traces of the island's times of elegance did remain, but the old houses were dilapidated, their grounds overgrown and untamed.

Although the area's man-made beauty was gone, its natural beauty had not been quelled. The Sea Islands of Georgia are actually a chain of barrier beaches that have grown over the centuries, miles of dunes and salt marshes that are almost empty of human habitation. Wild horses roam on deserted beaches; feral bulls crash through dense undergrowth; wild boars are not unknown; snowy egrets, once nearly extinct when their feathers were prized by ladies of fashion, compete with herons and ospreys for provender from the encircling waters; and alligators, as alligators do, go pretty much wherever they want and pretty much whenever they want to do it. There were insects too, lots of them, and every night the cicadas sounded as though they were mounting an invasion.

At the turn of the century, the Sea Islands' beauty was discovered by the great magnates of industry and finance, and they built huge mansions and elegant, exclusive private clubs; the local residents, descendants of freed African slaves, were valued for their labour and the food they pulled from the sea. But, other than that, their presence was mostly ignored. As Freda and Camilla travelled north, always staying as close to the sea as possible, Camilla often pointed out the old mansions and told baroque tales about their former inhabitants. Freda had her doubts about many of the fantastic events that Camilla chronicled – they sounded suspiciously like scenes from Fitzgerald's *The Great Gatsby* – but they made the ride pleasant and they were, if nothing else, fascinating.

Camilla was thoroughly enjoying herself. At one

point during the drive, she suddenly enthused, 'If Harold could only see me now!'

Freda pulled the car over and braked so fast Camilla had to clutch the door handle. 'What?' Freda demanded. 'Harold doesn't know where you are?'

Camilla dismissed the question with a wave of her hand. 'Oh, of course he does. I really meant, if he could see me now, carefree and devil-take-the-hindmost.'

It was an expression that Freda was not familiar with, but she ignored that for the moment. 'So, he'll be there in Toronto?'

Camilla sat up straighter. 'Certainly he will. I have only to telephone him upon my arrival and he will come and fetch me. After all, I *am* his mother!'

What the hell, Freda thought, forward, and she pulled the Thing out on to the road. Once again, Camilla had to grab the door handle.

While Freda and Camilla were driving north towards Fisherman's Island, Harold was on the set of his latest film, which, by coincidence, was set on a coastline. Exactly what coastline was not clear, because it was obvious that neither money nor care had gone into the set's construction, but it did provide a forum for the action and supported what little plot there was. As Harold watched, three women, naked from the waist up and wearing mermaid's tails from the waist down, were busy making love to a shipwrecked sailor who was obviously totally immersed in his role. The director was afraid that things would progress too far too soon, and he yelled, 'Cut!' There was no response from the actors, and the cameraman was too involved in the drama to stop the cameras.

'Hey!' the director yelled. 'That means *stop*!' That too produced no reaction, so the director hurried out on to the set and pulled the actors apart. 'Listen,' he told them. 'This isn't all action. You have to emote. I can't tell what you're thinking if you don't show it to me.'

One of the mermaids rolled her eyes, and another said something that the director didn't hear but it made the other actors laugh. Usually Harold would have been an active emotional participant in the making of the film, but he was distracted. He paced as he spoke to Vince on his cellular phone: 'It's not that I'm worried so much, but she could be lying on the kitchen floor.'

Vince said that he hadn't talked to Freda either. Harold turned and looked at the set. Why had the action stopped, he thought. Didn't the director know that time was money? 'Listen,' he said, without turning away from the actors, 'so, like, could you phone your wife and have her go over there and check on my mother and then call you back, and then you call me back here. Right?'

Vince agreed, and Harold clicked off without saying goodbye. 'What is it with these women that they're not answering the telephone?' he said, as the young woman who did the makeup approached. 'Telephones are for answering!'

The makeup woman decided to ignore the comment. 'Should I put nipple rouge on them?' she asked earnestly.

Harold didn't answer at first. After a minute, he said, 'Do you know that the myth of the mermaid was likely spawned by sailors looking at manatees?' The makeup woman seemed confused. 'That is to say, sea cows,' Harold elaborated, 'lying around on the shoreline?'

'Yeah? So?'

'So,' he said, raising his voice authoritatively, 'I'd say we need some nipple rouge.'

The makeup woman hurried off. Harold didn't even watch the application of the rouge. Instead, he called the house in Georgia again and again.

As the phone rang in the dark and empty house, Freda and Camilla were sitting on a dock eating shrimps.

As they sat there, swinging their legs over the side, they watched a heron sail smoothly across the road towards the ocean and, of course, Camilla had a relevant story. 'Once the Rajah of Bet-Ghee took me aboard his private yacht. His men had captured a sea hawk . . .'

Freda wanted to ask how they'd done that, but Camilla carried on.

'. . . they loaded its belly with gunshot, poured the pellets right down its gullet. Then they tied a hook around its neck and attached a long silver rope to its tail and released it upon the waters.'

Freda had no idea where this story was going, and she watched as a heron came back from the sea with a long fish hanging out of both sides of its beak.

Camilla was involved in her story, and she didn't see the heron. 'The great bird flew away . . .' She gestured wildly with her left arm, almost knocking a shrimp out of Freda's hand. '. . . the shot in its belly keeping it low to the waves. It flew for perhaps thirty feet, at which point a giant shark came out of the sea, taking the whole bird within its jaws.'

Camilla turned towards Freda. 'It took the men seven full hours to get the fish aboard,' she said, raising her voice a little for dramatic effect. 'It is amazing to reflect that the sea contained that magnificent creature. That life!'

'Yeah,' said Freda, nodding.

'I think that I would like to try my hand at fishing,' said Camilla.

'Fishing?' asked Freda. 'Where are we going to go fishing?'

'We must advance!' Camilla replied. 'We'll take the ferry.' She pointed ahead. Freda thought that Camilla had finally lost it. But she started the car, put it in gear and, after signalling and looking back carefully, she turned out into the empty road.

'Ferry?' she said when they were safely in motion. 'What ferry?'

'Leave that to me,' Camilla said, and, since by then there was only one road and no place to turn off, Freda had no choice. Soon enough, the road took them to a rickety old dock that led to a flat-decked boat that had obviously seen better days.

Freda stopped well short of the dock and the closed gate. '*That* is the ferry?' she asked. She wasn't sure she'd trust it to carry just herself and Camilla, let alone Vince's beloved Thing.

'Of course it is, girl.' Camilla pointed ahead. 'Forward!'

'I'm not so sure that's a good idea,' Freda said nervously.

'Of *course* it is. There have been ferries here since before you were born.'

'Well anyway, there's no one here to run it,' Freda observed.

Freda had discounted the man who was fishing off

the side of the boat. He hadn't moved since they'd been talking, and Freda assumed he was just using the boat as an extended dock. Freda, however, was wrong. The man, one Jerry Grantland, was, in fact, the 'captain', and also the owner of a magnificent, full-dress hangover, which the occasional sips of medicinal corn whiskey throughout the day had failed to dampen. 'Damn,' he said to himself, noticing his prospective passengers. Pulling himself to an upright position – not without consequence to his already aching head – he gathered up his fishing gear. 'Bastards!' he continued under his breath, and slowly walked on to the dock and up to the gate, opened it and unenthusiastically motioned Freda forward.

'You see,' Camilla said. 'I *told* you it was a ferry.'

I've gone this far, Freda thought, so I might as well go on, and she slowly drove the car on to the deck of the boat, and then she and Camilla got out. Camilla insisted on carrying her violin and carpet bag with her, which Freda found strange since they were only going to be fifteen feet away, but she said nothing. The women watched Mr Grantland walk slowly forward and pull an old, rusted chain across the end of the boat and then struggle to lock it in place with an equally old, rusted lock. In his impaired condition, he could not get the lock to work – it just wouldn't click – so finally he thought, the hell with it, and went back to the cubicle that held the wheel and the controls, where he put a ragged captain's cap on his head and started the engine. Even the engine protested, but in a minute or two, he was piloting the boat slowly out into the channel.

'Welcome aboard the *Seraph*, ladies and gentlemen,' he said, pausing for a moment, realizing that there were actually no gentlemen present, and then went on with his well-worn speech. 'This is your captain, Captain Grantland, speaking. Our voyage across takes approximately seven minutes.' He stopped speaking because he had to make a slight turn and had to concentrate.

'What'd he say?' Camilla asked loudly. It was difficult to hear over the noise of the engine, which had obviously seen better days.

Freda started to answer, but Captain Grantland launched back into his well-memorized speech. 'We ask at this time that you extinguish all smoking materials and make sure that the parking brake on your automobile is securely engaged.'

'What was that?' Freda asked.

'Something about a parking brake,' Camilla answered. Freda turned quickly towards the car, just in time to see it roll backwards, breaking through the flimsy chain as though it were a piece of string and fall off the boat and into the water. 'Oh no,' groaned Freda, and she raced to the end of the boat. The Thing had already vanished; all that remained were bubbles exploding upon the surface.

Camilla and the captain joined her, and they all watched the water in silence, as though by contemplation they could undo what had happened. Finally, the captain said, 'There's some hard luck for you.'

Freda mumbled something that no one could quite hear. 'I beg your pardon, dear,' Camilla said.

Freda pushed her hair back with both hands. This was indeed a bad situation. 'Well,' she said slowly, 'first of all I cursed. I cursed as only a woman who was raised with three brothers can. And furthermore, I'm going to say, ah, um, bastard.'

'Bastard!' Captain Grantland shouted in agreement. Now here was a woman he could communicate with! He was going to say it again, with even more feeling, but a particularly stern look from Camilla silenced him.

Freda felt the need to explain the profanity. 'I'm referring to Vince,' she said to Camilla, 'because this is his fault. Because he insists on keeping that piece of shit, even though the garage guy said its braking system was quote-unquote irredeemable.' Freda was getting upset now. First, because she was going to have to face Vince and explain this to him, and second, because, no matter what she thought about the Thing, it was, after all, a car, and it was currently on the bottom of some body of water that she didn't even know the name of. 'But no,' she continued, more loudly, 'in this one area of his life he is sentimental. And now all my stuff is at the bottom of the sea, and it's his fault. You hear me! His fault!'

Captain Grantland was not in any shape to deal with a hysterical woman, plus there was the small matter of his probably losing his job. 'We'll get this all sorted out,' he said quickly. God, his head hurt. 'There's no need to tell the police or my supervisor or any such bureaucratic bastard.'

'The police,' Camilla said thoughtfully. 'I once knew . . .'

'The only thing that course of action will do,' said Captain Grantland, 'is put an apple in old Jerry's butt and roast it up for supper.'

Camilla frowned at the vulgarism, but Freda ignored it. 'Hey, wait a sec,' Freda said.

'Yes?' said Camilla. She really didn't see why there

was all this concern about that atrocious vehicle. Her violin was the only really important thing, and she had that firmly in her hand.

'Just wait,' said Freda. She looked into the water as if she was waiting for something, and the others watched her watching the water. Finally she looked up. 'I guess none of that stuff floats, huh?'

'I wouldn't think so,' Captain Grantland said, and then he quickly continued: 'Here's my plan. I'll take you back to my place . . .'

'Perhaps we could hire deep-sea divers,' Camilla said, getting into the spirit of the situation.

'Never mind,' said Freda.

'Never mind?' Camilla had just started to enjoy tackling poor Freda's misfortune.

'Never mind,' said Freda firmly. 'When things sink, they're sunk, right?'

'My point exactly,' Captain Grantland quickly said. 'Things sink. That's not my fault. No one's fault, all right?'

'Perhaps we could get a submarine,' Camilla said thoughtfully.

'Listen,' Captain Grantland said. 'My name is Jerry. First, let me take you back to my place. We'll get it all sorted out there. It's the least I could do, take you home with me. After all, I suppose if I'd put on the padlock . . .' He suddenly realized what he'd said, and Freda did too.

'Padlock?' Freda asked.

'Reverse all engines!' Captain Grantland quickly shouted, and he went forward and pulled hard on the controls, creating enough noise so that no more conversation was possible. As the ferry returned to the dock, the women watched the place where the Thing had disappeared.

Evening was coming, and by the time they reached the dock it was cool, and Freda and Camilla were tired. They wanted to catch a bus out, but Jerry – he insisted that that they call him that, now that they were all friends – said there were no buses out until the next day so they'd have to spend the night at the old hotel where he lived. Actually, he wasn't exactly sure there were no buses, but he thought that keeping the ladies isolated might be a good idea in case they had second thoughts about not contacting the police or his boss or, even worse, someone from the local newspaper. Unfortunately, staying with Jerry involved crossing the same body of water that they'd started to cross on the ferry. And since there was absolutely no reason to waste the gasoline on the big boat, Jerry said they had to take a small motor boat. Neither of the women were enthusiastic about it, but within fifteen minutes they were bouncing across the bay, Freda and Camilla in the front, Jerry in the back coaxing as much energy as possible from the motor. Freda thought it sounded like a clothes dryer filled with scrap metal, and, after her previous experience, she had visions of being stranded in the boat, drifting across the water in the middle of the night.

'Are you sure there isn't a bus until tomorrow morning?' she called to Jerry, who was exhorting the engine under his breath.

'No fuss!' Jerry shouted back.

'Not *fuss*. Bus. *Bus!*' Freda said, but Jerry was intently involved with the motor, and Freda decided that it was probably best to let him do whatever it was he was doing, and she settled back and tried to enjoy the ride. It was quite cool on the water, and Freda pulled her knees up and hugged herself for warmth. After a minute or two, she relaxed a bit and watched Jerry work.

Up ahead, Freda saw a large building, like a castle, looming out of the evening fog. 'That's your place?' she asked him.

'No,' said Jerry. 'I just live there.'

As they drew closer, Freda saw that the building looked like a large old hotel, once grand but now in disrepair. Maybe, she thought, this won't be so bad after all, and she turned to look at Camilla, who gave her a big smile. It was obvious that Camilla considered this an Adventure, with a capital A, and she was enjoying every minute of it. What a character, Freda thought, and by then they were at the dock. Jerry helped them out of the boat and tried to take the violin case from Camilla, who clutched it tightly and gave Jerry a look that would have cowed a lesser – or at least a more sober – man. When they were firmly on land, Camilla took the lead towards the hotel, and Freda walked with her. Camilla had a power, a 'presence,' that Freda found enviable. Self-confidence was obviously integral to Camilla's life, and Freda wished that it was to her own.

'I've been here before,' Camilla told Freda as they walked. 'It was quite a resort in its day. The playing grounds of the rich and famous.' She lowered the pitch of her voice, but not the volume. 'It was here that Ivor used to bring his scrubbers and chippies.'

Jerry, who was walking just behind the women, was not sure what scrubbers and chippies were, but he knew from Camilla's tone that it wasn't nice. 'None of that now, ma'am,' he said quickly. 'It's been reputable for some time.'

'But *I* was faithful,' Camilla went on as though no one else had spoken. 'I travelled to all the cities of the world, and in each one there were a thousand men eager for the embraces of the great Camilla.

'I was always faithful, however. Faithful to a man who seduced every two-bit piece of baggage from here to California.'

'That was a long time ago,' Freda said gently.

'It was *not* a long time ago,' Camilla answered indignantly, as if the infidelities had occurred only a week or two ago. Then she stopped and said, 'It *was* a long time ago.' Freda put her arm around Camilla's shoulders and they walked on towards the steps of the hotel.

'You know,' Freda said, 'I really should try to call Vince.'

'Why would you do that?'

'You know, to tell him we're okay.'

'We're fine,' Camilla said. 'I guess it would be all right to give him a piece of your mind, though.'

Jerry escorted them inside, and Freda went to look for a telephone. The interior was still grand, in a faded sort of way. The original dark woodwork was still in place, and everything – the halls, the public rooms – was a little bit oversized. Camilla examined everything slowly, rubbing a finger over a piece of moulding, patting the back of an old chair.

Camilla was still examining her new surroundings when Freda returned. Freda shrugged and said, 'No one home. I had to leave a message on the machine.'

Camilla had always found answering machines distasteful, and she didn't like speaking about them.

'Still,' she said, 'I trust you gave him a royal earful.'

About what? Freda wondered. Then, she said, 'Oh sure. Mind you, I did drown the car, though.'

'I'm sure it deserved it,' Camilla said. 'I hear people,' she said to Jerry. 'Let us be announced.'

Chapter 8

During the year that it took Ewald to build his first violin, he also became a playmate of the young Camilla, which was the name she insisted he call her in private, even though it was not the name her parents used. Ewald thought that it was a bit strange – he thought *she* was a bit strange – but they did have a lot fun together. Their friendship started as a result of Camilla's mother needing some woodworking done in the house. Ewald's father had done a fine job on the sideboard he had repaired and, although Camilla's father thought that he charged much too much money, one afternoon, on the way back from Camilla's violin lesson, Camilla's mother stopped in the shop and asked Ewald's father if he could come with her to look at some things she wanted done. Ewald's father said of course he could, but he didn't want to leave the boy alone. 'Bring him along,' Camilla's mother said.

It was a great afternoon for the children. Camilla

showed Ewald her most secret treasures – some beautiful shells that had been brought from a South Pacific Island and a real Egyptian scarab – and Ewald tried to give Camilla his special pocketknife. Camilla didn't want the knife, but she reciprocated by playing the violin. Ewald was enchanted: he loved the sound of it, and he loved the way the instrument looked in Camilla's hands. He thought of the instrument he was building at the shop, and could hardly keep his secret. Even then, Ewald was fantasizing about running away with Camilla, running away to a far distant place where no one could find them and Camilla would play her violin.

Now, decades later, Ewald worked lovingly on what he thought might well be his last instrument. As he worked, Ewald wondered where Camilla was – if she was even still alive. He remembered the times he did try to convince Camilla to run away with him – times that started when they were both young and grew more serious as they got older. And he remembered the time they actually decided to do it, only to have Camilla change her mind at the last minute. He no longer faulted her for it; instead, it had become a bittersweet memory, softened and enhanced by the passage of time. And, as he remembered, his love for Camilla came flooding back as strongly as if it had all happened yesterday.

Chapter 9

It had turned into a fine evening; it was cool and the humidity was down. Harold and Vince did not notice the evening's beauty, however. When they had arrived at the airport an hour earlier, the only rental car available was a subcompact, which might have been adequate for Vince but which was not designed for a man of Harold's substantial proportions. The situation was not improved when Harold insisted on driving, because his driving matched his personality: aggressive and with little finesse. The situation was made even worse when Harold insisted on stopping for beer, which he drank while he drove, holding the steering wheel with one hand and a bottle with the other.

Neither man was in good shape when they reached the house. Harold had spent the entire drive listing his mother's faults, then feeling guilty and saying he hoped she wasn't dead on the floor somewhere, then saying that when he found her he was putting her in a home for sure this time. And when Harold wasn't complaining about his mother, he was complaining about the car. It required considerable effort for him to get himself out, and when he was finally on his feet in the driveway, he once again yelled, 'I reserved a Cadillac. What do I get, this damned Dinky toy!' He kicked the door and headed for the big house. When he stomped up the steps, he flung open the door and started yelling, 'Ma! Ma! Are you hiding again?'

There was no answer. Harold ran from room to room, expecting to find that his mother had finally gone to meet her Maker. When his search proved futile, he ran out to the cottage to see if Vince had found Freda. Vince had not only not found Freda, he knew that she didn't plan to come back because her guitar and all of her musical things were gone. Vince decided however, that, given Harold's obviously very anxious state, he'd keep that information to himself for a while. 'I'm sure they just went out for dinner or something,' he told Harold.

'Well, what do we do?' Harold said.

Vince figured that two or three more beers would calm Harold down considerably. 'How's the beer situation?' he asked.

'Beer?'

'Yeah, beer.'

'My mother's missing, and you want beer?'

'You got a better idea?' Vince asked.

Harold thought for a minute. 'Beer,' he finally agreed.

Camilla had an audience, and she loved it. Everyone in the hotel had gathered in the old salon, which was once a place only for conversation and music but now held a television as well. Camilla was at her effusive best, and for the first time in many months the television was dark and silent.

'I recall a certain occasion here on this island,' she told them. 'It was back in its heyday, back when it was populated by young Turks and their concubines.'

There was a whispering in the audience – did she mean people from Turkey? – and Camilla paused until it stopped.

'I challenged all the young roués to a tennis match. I played them all – Vanderbilt, Morgan, Kellog, Willie Dick – and I beat them, every one.'

While Camilla recited details about her opponents, always slipping in a spicy detail or two that was often about the men's 'playmates', Freda watched and listened. Camilla had become more alive, more vital. Did anything ever faze the woman, Freda wondered. Had Camilla ever had any doubts?

Camilla had finished dissecting the peccadilloes of the Vanderbilts *et al*, and then she turned her monologue to her husband. 'Of course, I was married at that time to Ivor. He insisted that he could do what no other man had been able to do: come to battle with me on the tennis court and emerge victorious. Ivor and I battled into the night. Neither one of us was prepared to give an inch. We played until the dawn came.'

Camilla paused, and then bent forward towards her audience, laughed and said, 'Ivor played well, but not well enough.'

Camilla had been telling stories for a long time, and, as an entertainer, which she surely was, she knew it was time for a change of pace. The room was quiet, but the damp evening air throbbed heavily with the rasping of the cicadas and occasionally a night bird of some kind called mournfully from the tree next to the windows. It was, in short, a beautiful evening, and Camilla felt *alive*: she was out of that dreadful old house; she was with people. Camilla is back, she thought, and she took Freda's hand and pulled her to her feet. 'Allow me to introduce my young companion,' she said.

'Camilla,' Freda whispered urgently. Freda didn't want to be introduced, and she had a bad feeling about whatever it was that Camilla was about to do.

Camilla ignored Freda's whisper completely and went on with her introduction. 'She has toured extensively throughout North America and the Continent with the famous group, the Backups.'

Oh no, Freda thought, and she noted that everyone was looking at her with new interest.

'She has composed many well-known songs,' Camilla continued. 'Ladies and gentlemen, Miss Freda . . .' Camilla stopped and whispered, 'Dear, what is your last name?'

Freda was nervous. And confused. 'Well, it's, um, my married name is Lopez, but my maiden name is Millson, so I think I should maybe use a hyphenate, you know, Millson-Lopez.'

'Too much talk, girl. Freda is sufficient,' Camilla said in a stage whisper. '*Mesdames et messieurs*,' she declaimed to the audience, 'the famous Freda.'

The people in the room applauded politely, some thinking that they'd heard the name someplace, and others thinking, who?

'Thank you,' Freda said nervously, 'but I'm not really famous, I . . .'

Camilla interrupted quickly, smiling at the audience. 'Many of Freda's finest . . .' she turned towards Freda and the smile was replaced with a stern look of warning, '. . . and most famous . . .' Camilla turned back towards the audience and smiled again, '. . . songs are the result of her bitter and tragic love affair with the handsome young artist Vincent.' Camilla turned back to Freda, extended her arm towards her, and said, 'Play us one of those songs, dear.'

Freda was still not comfortable with the deception and she started to explain to the audience. 'Vince is my husb – ' Camilla did not give her a chance to finish, but took her arm and led her to the piano. 'The great Camilla shall accompany you on the violin,' Camilla said, and she laid her violin case on the piano, took out her instrument and began to tune it. 'May I have an A, dear,' she said.

Freda was getting comfortable on the piano bench, and she looked up in confusion.

'A,' Camilla repeated.

Freda still didn't understand, and Camilla smiled at the audience and then reached out with one finger and gave the A above middle C a hard thump. She touched the strings on the violin and twisted the pegs a bit and said, 'Again, please.' This time, Freda gave her a solid A. Camilla smiled and nodded and then bent forward and whispered, 'Let us play for the plebs.'

Freda was beginning to get into the spirit of the moment. After not too much more hesitation, she began to play, firmly and decisively, one of her songs, a sultry, syncopated piece of parlour music that Camilla had coached her on. She played it once through and then began again, this time with more feeling. The women were playing only for themselves and for each other, for lost dreams, for real or imaginary past triumphs, for the future, and, ultimately, for the love of the music itself. When they were finished, the small audience was quiet, not quite realizing what had happened but knowing that it was something special. Then they applauded and shouted, 'Encore!' Freda was ready to play again, but Camilla whispered, 'Always leave them wanting more,' and she put her violin in its case and Freda understood and closed the piano lid and stood. After a few minutes the women left, Freda to walk around outside for a while and Camilla to go upstairs and get prepared for bed, which, for Camilla, was a lengthy and elaborate process.

While the rest of the residents and guests were still sitting together talking about their strange and wonderful new visitors, Camilla and Freda were getting into bed. They shared a room, and Freda watched with amusement while Camilla took an extra pair of pyjamas from the carpet bag and, after she put them on, washed out the dress she was wearing. Outside, a particularly loud cicada rasped from a limb near their window, and there was a crash somewhere nearby as an alligator tipped over a garbage can. Freda, however, noticed none of the sounds of the night. She was still elated with the thrill of performing.

'So, I was okay?' she asked.

Camilla sat up in her bed. '"Okay" is a word to use if someone asks you if you want another cup of coffee. It is not a word to apply to a musical performance. You tell me how you were, girl.'

'Well,' said Freda, 'I was, uh, magnificent.'

'Naturally you were. You are an accomplished performer.' Camilla spoke as if she were tutoring a slightly slow pupil.

'Come off it!' Freda laughed, but it was a sour laugh, not one of amusement.

'What?'

'Listen,' said Freda. 'I'm not an accomplished anything. Least of all a performer. If you hadn't been there I would have . . .' Freda remembered some of the things Camilla had said in her introduction and then she started to laugh again, this time without any sourness. '"Her bitter and tragic love affair with the handsome artist Vincent!" Hey, it's not *that* tragic.'

'I'd say it's pretty tragic,' said Camilla. 'I married Ivor when I was seventeen. He died when I was fifty-three. The arithmetic escapes me, but that's a goddamned long time to be locked in a loveless marriage.' Camilla firmly pulled the covers up to her chin.

'I don't think Vince and I have a loveless marriage.'

'Oh, is that what you don't think?' Camilla was silent for a moment, lost in the past. 'Well, you keep telling yourself that. It seems to help.'

Freda did not answer, but she turned out the light and then got into her own bed in the dark. She was asleep within minutes, but Camilla lay awake on her back, staring at the ceiling she could not see and remembering a handsome young violin maker, the one who'd made the instrument that was on the table by her bed.

While Freda and Camilla were settling in for the night, Harold and Vince were sitting at Camilla's kitchen table surrounded by empty beer bottles; a few, unnoticed, had even fallen to the floor. Vince had been talking about baseball, and Harold knew that Vince had missed a vital point. 'Excuse me!' Harold interrupted. 'Excuse me! The designated hitter is a blight upon the face of the universe.'

'Oh right,' Vince answered sarcastically. 'I know I'd much rather watch some pitcher who's got a one-twenty-six average strike out.'

'Ah!' Harold said triumphantly. 'But should you stop and analyse the statistics, you'd find the difference in . . .'

The absurdity of the conversation finally penetrated Vince's alcoholic haze, and he interrupted. 'I'll tell you the truth, Harold. I don't give a damn about the designated hitter.'

'Me neither,' Harold admitted. He started pulling at the label on a beer bottle and was quiet until he had the entire label off in one piece. 'Well, my mom's finally done it. She's run away from home.'

Vince tried to be reasonable. 'Look, they're two grown women.'

'Listen,' said Harold. 'When my mom's not in the house I get very nervous, and that means soon I'm going to have an anxiety attack.'

Vince nodded, not really listening. He was wondering if this was in fact the end of his and Freda's marriage.

'Listen,' Harold said, grabbing Vince's hand. 'Do you know what to do if I have an anxiety attack? Make me breathe into a paper bag.'

Now Harold's sounding crazy, Vince thought; it must run in the family. 'I'm sure they'll be home any minute,' he said slowly and calmly.

Harold had always pictured himself as a man of

action, and he decided that now was time. 'I'm calling the police,' he said suddenly, and he stood up so quickly his chair fell over, which made Vince jump.

'What police?' Vince asked. If there was a local police force, he'd seen no evidence of it.

'The state police,' Harold said decisively. He picked up the telephone, dialled 0, and barked, 'Get me the police!' and asked Vince, 'What's the licence number on that piece-of-shit car?'

'Hey!' Vince protested. 'That car is almost an antique. I love that car!'

Harold listened to the operator. 'The state police, of course!' he replied, almost shouting. The operator said something that Harold didn't like, but before he could reply she'd made the connection and the phone was ringing in the local state police headquarters.

When the call was answered, Harold said, trying to sound as calm as possible, 'I'd like to report a missing person.'

Camilla and Freda slept soundly that night. Both of them dreamed of performing, and when the morning came they were refreshed. It was a clear, beautiful morning, and the onshore breeze rustled the lace curtains and filled the room with the smell of the sea, which gave Camilla an idea. 'Why don't you go have your breakast, girl,' she said. 'I've got things to do.'

'What things?' Freda asked suspiciously.

'Just things,' said Camilla. 'When you get to be my age it takes a little more to get you running in the mornings.'

'Okay,' said Freda. She was still not convinced that Camilla didn't have another crazy scheme, but there didn't seem to be too many ways Camilla could get into trouble there, and besides, Freda was hungry, very hungry. She wondered if it was the salt air.

Freda ate her breakfast on the wrap-around veranda. When she'd finished and Camilla still had not appeared, she took a walk around the grounds. Obviously, they'd once been magnificent, but they had lacked care for many years and the trees and shrubs, no longer pruned, had gone wild. As Freda examined a large magnolia that, she thought, might have been as much as a century old, a couple of local girls, probably ten or eleven years old, stood a bit away watching Freda with admiration. Finally one of them got the courage to come closer and talk. 'Are you famous?' she asked.

'Me?' said Freda. 'No.'

The girl could think of nothing else to say, and Freda could see that she was very disappointed. 'Not all over the world, anyway,' Freda added. 'Only in, um, North America. And Europe, of course.'

The girl that had held back heard this and came closer. 'Wow,' she exclaimed.

Freda warmed to her audience. 'And of course, there was the Australian tour. A stunning success. Fifty thousand Maoris came from the Outback just to see me.'

The girl was not sure who the Maoris were or what the Outback was, though she thought that since 'Outback' sounded something like 'Outhouse' it wasn't very nice, so she quickly changed the subject. 'Do you know Madonna?'

Freda looked away from the girls for a second and saw Camilla heading towards the water from the back of the hotel. She was dressed in men's clothes, and was carrying a huge surf-casting rod.

'Sure,' said Freda, 'skinny blonde girl,' and she hurried to catch Camilla.

'Wow!' the girl said, again, after Freda left.

Freda ran across the lawn and caught up with Camilla as she was about to cross the road, beyond which lay the beach. 'Hi,' she said.

Camilla didn't stop. 'Jerry tells me there's a huge school of bluefish going by. Isn't that wonderful?' She stopped and then looked at Freda. 'Oh,' she said, 'but you wanted to hurry back to Savannah, didn't you?'

What the hell, Freda thought. 'No big rush,' she said.

'Fine,' Camilla said. 'To the sea!'

The road separating them from the ocean had been mostly abandoned years ago. It was scarred and filled with pot holes; occasionally something green sprouted from a crack in the pavement, and as they crossed Camilla observed, 'This highway needs attention.' On the other side, they came to a grid of rusted, moss-encrusted iron bars spaced about two inches apart. They had to cross the bars to reach the beach. 'What is this?' Camilla asked.

Freda looked down and was suddenly flooded with memories from her childhood. 'It's a Texas gate,' she said.

'And what might be the purpose of this arrangement?'

'There must've been cows here sometime,' said Freda. 'I suppose this was to keep them from going out to sea.'

'How?' Camilla asked. She never remembered any cows on the island, but she decided to let that pass for the moment.

'Let's say I'm a cow,' Freda told her.

'Right, you're a cow.'

Freda slumped over and curved her hands and held them to her head in a representation of horns. She pantomimed walking along the road, stopping to look at bits of edible greenery here and there, and finally reaching the Texas gate. When she saw it, she shrank back and then tried again, but after several tries she still couldn't find the courage to cross and she resumed her meander down the road. 'You see? Cows won't go over it. There's this thing about cows. They're cautious. Even though it wouldn't break their legs or anything, they still won't cross it.'

'Isn't that silly of the clever things,' Camilla said, and she stepped, a little gingerly, across the gate. 'Come, girl, the fish won't wait.'

Camilla tried hard to look as if she'd been fishing all of her life, but it was obvious to Freda after a few minutes that if Camilla had ever held a fishing rod in her life it had been a long time ago. Camilla struggled hard, but she couldn't get the plug that Jerry had already attached to the end of the wire leader far enough out into the water to attract anything but the minnows swept into the shallows by the current. It didn't seem to bother Camilla though, and as she flung the rod about she said, 'I've been trying to remember this poem.' And she began to recite: 'I must down to the seas again/To the vagrant gypsy life/To the gulls way.'

'There,' said Freda, 'you've remembered it.'

'No, there's more,' said Camilla, looking slightly irritated that she couldn't get the rest.

Freda decided it was time to give some friendly fishing advice, and as Camilla brought the rod up again, Freda said, 'You want to let the line go when the rod's at about one o'clock.'

A gull passed low overhead and screeched at them as Camilla thought, who is this girl to be giving me advice. 'What would you know about it?' she asked.

'When he wasn't farming, my dad took me fishing,' Freda told her.

Camilla held the rod still for a moment and thought about that. 'Very well,' she said, and she cast again, this time watching the tip of the rod and carefully releasing the line at exactly the right time. The cast was perfect, though Camilla didn't thank Freda for the advice.

It was an almost perfect day, warm but not hot. There was a mild onshore breeze that was refreshing, and Freda enjoyed it while she watched Camilla cast again and again. For a moment, Freda thought about Vince, and knew that soon she'd have to call him, but then she abandoned herself to the beauty of the day and just revelled in being alive. Her thoughts then turned to her childhood, growing up on a farm in the Canadian midwest. It had been a serene, almost idyllic childhood, but Freda had always felt sorry for the cows, although they too had a pretty good life. 'You know,' she said, 'one night when I was a little girl I tried to set all my father's cows free.'

'Freda, the Great Bovine Emancipator,' Camilla proclaimed, casting again.

'I let them all out of the barn, I let them out of

the stock pens, I herded them up from all over the property, but I couldn't get them past the Texas gate. Stupid cows!'

'Indeed,' Camilla agreed. 'Why didn't you just . . .' There was suddenly a hard jerk on her line, and Camilla yelled, 'Eureka!' The rod twisted and bent and seemed to have a life of its own.

'"Eureka"?' Freda laughed. 'I've never heard that one before. I've heard "I've got a strike." I've heard "fish on". I've even heard "I nailed the bastard." But never "Eureka".'

Boy, that girl can be annoying sometimes, Camilla thought. 'Don't mock me, young woman,' she said. 'This fish is battling very valiantly indeed.'

Freda laughed and decided it was time to give Camilla a little more advice. 'Keep the rod tip up, Camilla. Rod tip up! Keep the tension on the line. We're going to land this baby.'

I'm going to land this baby, Camilla thought.

It was a painting: an old woman reeling in a fish with an extremely long rod that was bent at its tip; a young woman watching and giving encouragement; blue-green sea under blue sky, white sand that faded into the sky in the distance. Camilla did it all herself and finally, when she had the fish in the shallows, Freda waded into the water. The fish feinted and darted and tried to get away from Freda, but Freda followed the fish's jerky movements with her hand just above the water and then, with an impressive display of dexterity, plunged her hand into the water and grabbed the fish just behind the tail and held it up for Camilla to see. It was a good-sized bluefish, but Freda was sure that over the next few days, as Camilla told the story, the fish would gain fifty pounds and a couple of feet. 'Ta da!' said Freda.

'My goodness gracious. What a large fish he is,' Camilla exclaimed proudly.

'It's probably a she,' Freda told her. 'In the fishy kingdom, it's the females that get big.'

'Then we just let her go,' Camilla said.

Freda held the fish up and looked at Camilla for a moment as if to say, really? Then she agreed. 'Okay, give me some slack,' said Freda. 'Just flip open the bail, and you can put the rod down.'

'Bail?' Camilla examined the mechanism of the reel.

'Just flip that little lever on the side.'

'Check,' said Camilla, and she released the line and put the rod on the sand. Freda gently pulled the lure from the fish's mouth and then held it in the water for a moment until it struggled to get free. Then she let it go, and in an instant it was gone.

'Goodbye, fishy,' Freda called, and she turned back to the beach to see Camilla undressed to her elaborate undergarments, which she was in the process of also taking off.

'*What* are you doing?' Freda exclaimed.

'Going for a dip,' Camilla told her, and by then she was naked and heading for the water.

'Wait for me!' Freda yelled, and she ran out and pulled her clothes off, and in two minutes the two were skinnydipping in the ocean. Camilla was singing at the top of her lungs, and finally Freda asked what it was she was singing.

'Why the Brahms,' said Camilla. 'You do remember the Brahms, don't you, girl? We're going to hear the Brahms!'

Indeed we are, Freda said to herself. 'You know,' she told Camilla, 'as Vince would say, you're cool.'

Camilla stood on the bottom for a moment, then started to leave the water. 'Let us not talk of unpleasant things. And I'm not cool, I'm cold!'

Vince, Freda thought, I really should call him.

Chapter 10

Camilla first heard the Brahms Violin Concerto when she was ten or eleven. The student before her – a young man in his twenties – was having an exceptionally good lesson and Herr Professor Schoen allowed it to run long, with Camilla sitting there listening. Camilla didn't know what the piece was, but she thought she had never heard anything so beautiful. When she opened the door and the Professor motioned her to come in and sit, the violinist was playing a complicated solo passage, and then, when it came to its quiet end, the Professor joined in, playing the orchestra part on the piano. The next minutes were so beautiful it brought tears to Camilla's eyes; she thought it sounded like an angel singing. Then, when Camilla was already overcome by the beauty of the music, the Professor and the student started the second movement.

The movement opens with the orchestra, but the Professor played the part on the piano, caringly and with great love, while the student held his violin at his side. When the violin finally came in, Camilla listened to the slow, simple melody for a couple of minutes and then broke down into tears.

That stopped the lesson, of course. The Professor offered Camilla the sharply pressed white handkerchief that he always kept in his jacket pocket, and while she was using it he dismissed the other student and left Camilla alone for a minute or two. When he came back into the room, Camilla was sitting on the piano bench with the score in her hands.

'Who was Br-aah-ms?' she said carefully.

'Brahms,' the Professor corrected gently, and he explained who the composer had been.

'I want to learn this,' Camilla said.

The Professor had been amused by Camilla's emotion but had been careful not to show it. Now, however, he laughed aloud. Camilla was a mediocre student, and she was terrified of performing. He didn't see the Brahms concerto in her future. 'That's too big a piece for a little girl,' he said. 'Maybe in ten years,' he told her, thinking, never.

The Professor was the first of many men throughout Camilla's life who would seriously underestimate her determination. Camilla got her mother to buy the music for her that very day after her lesson, and when she got home she started to study it. Just its appearance brought her to tears again, and this time they were tears of frustration. She had never seen most of the notation and had no idea what it meant; there were notes in the score that she had not known the violin was capable of playing; there were actually places where the violin played two notes at once, which she *knew* she'd never be able to play; and worst of all, there were no fingerings or bowings in the score, and she'd never had to figure out those things for herself.

Nevertheless, within a week she could play the first few bars of the violin part of the second movement – the slow one that had affected her so much at the Professor's. She worked on the movement for four months, never telling the Professor what she was doing. Finally, when she thought she was ready, she first played the movement for her friend Ewald, who promptly asked her to marry him. Camilla was flattered and a little embarrassed. 'Don't be silly,' she told him.

Then the day of her lesson arrived, and she was so nervous that she was sick to her stomach and her mother told her she would have to skip her lesson that week.

'No!' Camilla said, and with a tremendous strength she willed herself not to be sick any more. Her mother didn't think the lesson was a good idea that day, but Camilla insisted. Two hours later, she was at the door of the Professor's studio. She took a big breath and told her mother she'd see her in an hour. Walking in, she said, 'Good afternoon' to the Professor, removed her coat, took out her copy of the Brahms concerto, opened it to the second movement, put it on the piano rack, and took out her violin and tuned it. The Professor was amused by the drama, and didn't even get out of his chair to see what piece Camilla had placed on the music rack. He just said, 'Let's begin,' expecting to hear the little baroque piece he had assigned.

And then the young Camilla started the second movement of the Brahms with that combination of fervour and innocence that only the young can bring to music. The Professor had never heard a performance of the movement like it, from anyone of any age, and as she played he moved quietly to the piano and took up the orchestra part, and when they finished the movement the Professor could not speak because he knew if he opened his mouth he would cry.

Camilla thought that she'd played well, but as the Professor's silence grew longer she was afraid that she'd done terribly. Finally, she could stand it no longer. 'Was it okay?' she asked. The Professor could only nod while two big tears rolled down his cheeks.

Three-quarters of a century later, Ewald was carving the neck of the last violin he would make. He took extra care with it. Under his fingers from the wood emerged the most graceful and delicate scrollwork he had ever done. While he worked, he thought of Camilla and that slob of a husband of hers, a large man, ten years older than Camilla, much taken with strong drink, large cigars, and bawdy tales, a man who had treated Ewald's Camilla as an elegant possession to be shown off to his friends, all of whom were similar men. Even so many years later, the thoughts made Ewald angry and his chisel slipped a bit. He put it down and took up a piece of sandpaper and gently sanded away the slight imperfection. But when he was ready to carve again, he couldn't get Camilla's husband out of his mind. So he put his work away, closed his workshop and went into his music room where he put on a recording of the Brahms. As he listened, he saw the beautiful young Camilla.

Chapter 11

Harold and Vince were suffering from the effects of too much beer and too little sleep. They had telephoned police headquarters the night before, sometime after midnight, obviously waking a young state trooper named Kapur, who asked them to come to the station where they could start getting to the bottom of this mysterious disappearance.

On the drive up the coast, Harold was in a foul mood. Hungover and still complaining about the size of the rental car, he was also clearly angry with Vince.

'It wasn't too much to ask,' fumed Harold. 'It's a simple procedure. The kitchen is full of paper bags.'

'I said I was sorry,' replied Vince. 'I didn't realize you were having an anxiety attack.'

'I answer the telephone. Suddenly, I turn bright red, I start panting, sweat comes out of my eyeballs and you don't recognize these as symptoms of distress?'

Vince was in no mood to argue. His head hurt and

although he usually found Harold's hysteria amusing, right now it was merely exhausting.

'My wife is missing,' he said. 'I have my own problems, okay?'

They pulled up to the ferry docks, where various squad cars were parked here and there, just in time to see Vince's Thing being winched out of the water. For Vince, it was indeed a low point: his beloved vehicle dangling helplessly on a hook, like a tired and humiliated old fish.

Harold spotted someone who seemed to be in charge, a slight but well-groomed state trooper, apparently East Indian, who was sporting an oversized hat that looked not unlike a cowboy's ten-gallon special. This, it turned out, was Kapur. Although Vince was still feeling queasy from the sight of his poor, waterlogged Thing, he walked right up to the officer and fired the first question.

'Have you organized a search party?' he asked.

'Uh, no,' replied Kapur. 'But that's a pretty good idea.'

Harold was already thinking the worst. 'If, God forbid, they'd drowned, would their bodies get washed up on shore or what?'

'Well, I'm not sure,' answered Kapur calmly, standing with his thumbs tucked down the front of his belt. 'I suppose eventually. But I don't think anyone in that car drowned, provided they could swim.'

'Ma can swim,' Harold volunteered quickly.

'Sure, Freda can too,' added Vince. 'But hold on, what was my car doing on the bottom of the ocean?'

'Well, I have some theories about that,' stated Kapur proudly.

'Jeez, a regular Sherlock Holmes,' muttered Vince, sarcastically. Vince was already doubting the abilities of this state trooper, who looked for all the world like a pint-sized John Wayne wannabe.

'Very well, gentlemen,' said Kapur indignantly, 'I'll go organize a posse.'

'Not a posse,' barked Vince. 'A search party.'

'Right, a search party,' said Kapur, nodding his head. And he set off to round up a group of police officers and some locals – curious onlookers who'd gathered at the site when news of the sunken car first spread.

Harold was perspiring profusely in the hot noonday sun, so he sat down on a shaded tree stump and, with a large white handkerchief taken from his back pocket, wiped his worried, sweaty brow. Stay calm, he told himself. The last thing you need to have out here is another anxiety attack.

The rag-tag search party, meanwhile, had begun striking their way, half-heartedly, through the bush. Vince, following a few steps behind Officer Kapur, lit up a cigarette and offered one to the state trooper, who politely declined.

'You don't think this search party is such a good idea, do you?' said Vince, somewhat rhetorically.

'Frankly, Mr Lopez,' said Kapur, 'I don't. Very few people are actually lost.'

'What do you mean?'

'I mean, Mr Lopez, isn't it possible your wife is running away from you?'

'No,' said Vince, obviously not having given the matter a moment's thought.

'You have a perfect marriage, Mr Lopez?' asked Kapur bluntly.

'Well, come on, is anything that simple?' replied Vince. 'Can anyone say they have a perfect marriage?'

'I can,' said Kapur firmly. Then, looking over at his search party, he shouted, 'Hey, y'all!' in his best Texas accent. 'I love saying that,' he gushed to himself as he and Vince approached Harold. Now it was Kapur's turn to be sarcastic. 'Hey, y'all! Check out down that culvert! Climb down into all that muck and crap and see if you can't find this guy's wife!'

'Forget it,' said Vince, not wanting to be made a fool of by this police officer. 'Never mind.'

'Come, Mr Cara,' said Kapur, turning to the still-seated and sweating Harold. 'Let's go to the station.'

The police station seemed to be a one-man operation, and Officer Kapur was proudly showing off his brand new computer, which he boasted was the answer to all their problems, a machine capable of interfacing with every law enforcement agency in the country. Now, if only he could lay his hands on the instruction booklet . . .

While Harold and Vince were growing impatient with this novice techno-buff and his new toy, Camilla and Freda were setting off from Fisherman's Island, ready to resume their travels to Toronto. After Jerry dropped them off at the mainland – just a short distance, in fact, from the police station – they waved goodbye and were lucky to catch the only bus heading north that afternoon.

The bus, a rickety old contraption that bounced along the dusty coastal roads without benefit of shock absorbers, seemed to stop at every hamlet on the route

– despite being called the Chattanooga Express, and much to the annoyance of Camilla.

'It's the milk run,' Freda explained, using an expression from her rural past.

'Why didn't you lay down a board?' asked Camilla, in typical non-sequitur fashion.

'What?'

'For the cows,' Camilla said. 'Why didn't you just lay down a large board, hiding those frightening bars from sight, thereby allowing them to cross over?'

'Because I never thought of it, that's why,' Freda replied, a tad testily. 'Why didn't you tell Ivor and his chippers to go to hell?'

'They're not called chippers, they're called chippies,' Camilla corrected. 'Besides,' she added with a huff, 'it simply wasn't done. Why don't *you*, now that it's common as toadstools?'

'I don't *want* to leave my husband,' Freda insisted.

Camilla, as usual, got the last word. 'Oh, but you *have* left your husband, dear,' she said. 'It's going back that we're talking about.'

Before Freda had a chance to stew over that one, the bus pulled into a truckstop and lurched to a halt. This was as far north as the Chattanooga Express was going. From here on, Freda and Camilla would have to find another method of transportation. But now they were hungry, and this restaurant, though hardly a fine dining establishment, would have to do.

As they entered, Camilla told Freda to go on ahead, implying that she had to use the ladies' room or some such, and asked Freda to order her a cheeseburger, which puzzled Freda a little. 'Okay,' said Freda.

Camilla found what she was looking for: a payphone.

Reaching down the front of her dress, she removed a small change purse and took out a quarter. A small boy, who'd witnessed Camilla's deft extraction, stood nearby, slack-jawed.

'That's right, son,' she told him, as she went to make her call. 'That's what all the secrecy's about. We have money down there.' The boy walked off, in wide-eyed wonder.

The restaurant, a typical greasy-spoon, was noisy and smoky and full of large-bellied men in grubby T-shirts and what appeared to be, mostly, Caterpillar caps.

Freda, carrying a tray with cheeseburgers, weaved her way around the tables, looking for a place to sit. Finally, she spotted a table for four, occupied by a single man.

'Excuse me, could my friend and I sit here?' she asked. 'There's no free tables.'

The man, unlike others in the truckstop, was cleanly dressed, handsome and, judging by the hardcover book he was reading – a biography on Gandhi – even somewhat cultured.

'Absolutely,' he said, and stood up in a gracious show of old-world charm. 'Please, I insist!'

Freda smiled, shyly, and thanked him. As she sat down, she decided that the occasion called for some polite chit-chat. 'Good book?' she inquired.

'Not bad. The author is not one hundred per cent clear on all his facts, but then again, who is really?'

'That's true,' replied Freda tentatively, thinking it a curious response to give a total stranger. As she wondered which way to take the conversation next, Camilla arrived and congratulated Freda on finding a table.

'This is my friend, Camilla Cara,' said Freda.

'*The* Camilla Cara,' Camilla added, in her usual theatrical style.

'Oh yes, yes,' said the man, smiling genially and pretending to recognize the name. 'And I am Hunt Weller.'

'Freda Millpez,' offered Freda, suddenly deciding to create a hybrid of her maiden and married names.

'Liked enemas,' interjected Camilla, stabbing a finger at Weller's book.

'What's that?' asked Weller, not at all catching her drift.

'One of Gandhi's little quirks,' Camilla continued. 'Liked to give them to his close friends. But I refused. I said, "No, no, Mahatma . . ."'

'Let's eat,' said Freda quickly, wanting to change the subject before Camilla got any further into scatological territory. 'Excuse me, Mr Weller,' Freda said, 'do you know if there's a train station nearby?'

'I'm afraid we've misplaced our peculiar automobile,' added Camilla, jumping in.

'It's Hunt,' Weller insisted. 'And where are you heading?'

'North,' said Freda.

Weller smiled, looked meaningfully across the table at both women and said, 'I, myself, am headed north. Why don't I just pop off and get us a car?' As he said this, he promptly stood up with his book and left, leaving behind his lunch bill.

Within minutes, the three were cruising north through Tennessee in a luxurious black Buick convertible. Camilla sat in the back and soaked up the sun's rays. Freda, riding up front, was also enjoying herself, as if the forward motion of the car alone represented the progress she was seeking in her life. Weller, meanwhile, personified that devil-may-care feeling. As Freda watched him behind the wheel, his long pony-tail flapping in the breeze, she wondered what this carefree sophisticate did for a living.

Just then, Camilla leaned forward and struck up a conversation with Weller. 'Do you know we're travelling with a famous musician?' she told him.

'Camilla,' said Freda crossly, wanting to nip this subject in the bud.

'Freda got very tired of performing after a while,' Camilla continued. 'What a grind, though. It is a grind, isn't it dear?' she said, turning to Freda in an attempt to engage her.

'Sure,' Freda allowed.

'The touring especially,' Camilla continued. 'Every day a new city. So . . .?'

'Okay,' said Freda, picking up Camilla's cue. 'So, I thought I'd do some recording – just simple stuff, four-track, grass roots. You know, bass, piano.'

Weller's face contorted in disgust, as if Freda had just said something distasteful.

'What?' Freda asked.

'So many people send me tapes,' began Weller, 'and when I hear that instrumentation, I think retro. You know? Technology's exploding, technology's having an intergalactic orgasm, and yet people proffer product that is essentially medieval.'

The wind had been taken out of Freda's sails, and she was momentarily speechless. Catching her breath, she ventured, 'People send you tapes?'

'My staff weeds out the real dross,' allowed Weller,

puffing out his chest a little. 'I only listen to the best of it, and none of it's much good, frankly.'

'Are you a producer or something?' Freda asked.

Weller let out a chortle. 'A producer or something! I love it.'

'Should I have heard of you?'

'Yes,' answered Weller bluntly. He then ended the inquisition by asking Camilla whether she would appreciate a cup of tea.

'I would, indeed, young man,' Camilla replied.

'So be it,' said Weller, turning off on to a small road that led towards a large, stately manor.

As Freda and Camilla stood on the veranda, admiring the spacious grounds and sniffing in the fragrant scent from a row of magnolia trees, Weller fumbled about in his back pocket, evidently searching for a key. He found one under a flowerpot to one side of the door, and escorted the two women in.

Weller led them into a parlour room, elegantly decorated with wainscoting and a massive white marble fireplace. In the middle of the room stood a grand piano, to which Freda immediately gravitated. Weller, obviously pleased that things were going so swimmingly, told the ladies to make themselves at home while he rustled up some tea.

After he left the room, Camilla looked at Freda. 'A little fling before you turn yourself in,' she said, grinning.

'What do you mean, turn myself in?' asked Freda.

'That's what you said,' Camilla reminded her. '"We'll go to Toronto," you said, "and I'll turn myself in." So this is your last huzzah.'

Having finally laid his hands on the instruction manual

for his new computer, Kapur was busy getting himself acquainted with its operation. 'Congratulations on selecting the Bicon X-50,' he read out loud from the booklet, 'the technology that makes law enforcement so easy it's a crime.' Kapur chuckled.

Vince and Harold were not amused, however, and they glared at the state trooper. Too many coffees and an excess of sugary crullers had left the pair edgy and irritable. Vince paced nervously about the station, while Harold cleaned his fingernails with a Bugs Bunny letter-opener Kapur had picked up on a family trip to Disneyworld.

'Shouldn't we be doing something?' asked Vince, finally breaking the silence.

'Yes,' said Harold. 'Why don't you phone your place and see if your wife has left any messages.'

'Good idea,' said Vince, who quickly grabbed a telephone. He was about to dial when he asked, 'How exactly do I do that? I forgot my access code.'

Kapur, meanwhile, squealed with delight at finally getting some sign of life on his computer screen.

'Myself, I've got a service,' Harold told Vince, picking up another phone and dialling a number. 'I've got people I can talk to. I appreciate the *human* touch.' Much to Harold's satisfaction, his call was quickly answered by a service operator, Marge, the same one he'd been dealing with for two years.

'Cara, here,' he said, picking up a pencil. 'Ready? Shoot.' He began scratching out his messages. 'Got it,' he said, taking down the first one. 'Uh-huh. Jerry or Stanley Rose?' The operator didn't know. 'Well, you have to *ask*!' he hollered. 'You *have* to ask! Okay, okay.'

Some touch, thought Vince.

Harold asked the operator to continue. 'Anything else? KME Films. Got it. Next. 'Your mother has been . . .' I beg your pardon? What is this, a joke?' Harold, suddenly bug-eyed and ashen-faced, lowered the phone.

'My mother's been kidnapped,' he said weakly, stricken with panic.

Without a moment's hesitation, Vince picked up a Dunkin' Donuts bag and placed it directly over Harold's face.

'It's going to be allright, Mr Cara,' said Kapur. 'What else did they say?'

'That they would call later,' gasped Harold through the bag, which was puffing out and retracting like a bullfrog's throat in full croak.

'What about Freda,' asked Vince. 'Did they say anything about Freda?'

Harold, or rather Harold's donut bag, merely shook back and forth, indicating that they hadn't.

Chapter 12

Under Herr Professor Schoen's astute instruction, Camilla blossomed into both a musical prodigy and something of a local sensation. Her recitals at Toronto's Royal Conservatory of Music began drawing aficionados from across the city who came to hear Schoen's gifted young student. Her reputation grew to the point where Clyde Witherspoon, classical music critic for the *Toronto Telegram*, predicted that this 'new princess of the violin' was destined for an illustrious career on the world's finest stages.

Camilla's role with the Professor soon evolved into something more than a simple student–teacher relationship. Their lessons usually began with Camilla playing her homework, that is to say, demonstrating what she'd learned between lessons. And they almost always ended up with Camilla and the Professor performing advanced duets for violin and piano, often running well past the one-hour instruction time.

Soon, Camilla's lessons increased to three times a week.

Meanwhile, her relationship with Ewald also became more complex. What started out as an innocent childhood friendship grew into an agonizing teenage romance. Ewald's feelings for Camilla, of course, had always been strong. And while they were both still quite young, he had surprised her with the gift of his first handmade violin; although it was somewhat crudely constructed, Camilla had been deeply touched by the gesture.

It was only when Camilla turned fourteen that she began to look upon Ewald as something more than a friend. The change took place one day in August, when the two of them, still off from school, were seeking some relief from a heat wave. Lying to her parents, who disapproved of her growing intimacy with a working-class, immigrant boy, Camilla arranged to meet Ewald at the city docks, where they caught a ferry over to Hanlan's Point, a popular beach on the Toronto Islands. There, after a picnic on the sand and a swim in the lake, Ewald startled Camilla with a sudden kiss.

Actually, it was more of a miss than a kiss; unsure, initially, of his intentions, Camilla had let out a nervous laugh just as Ewald was leaning in, causing his lips to meet her squarely on the teeth. But rather than become a source of embarrassment or awkwardness, the amorous attempt endeared Ewald to Camilla, who began to see in the handsome teenage boy a sensitive young man with whom, she felt, she could share almost anything.

And, indeed, they shared many things for the next few years. Mostly, it was their love of music and instruments. They dreamed of a future where Camilla played with leading orchestras in cities all over the world. And they fantasized about how Ewald would one day become an internationally famous violin maker.

They saw less of each other during the school year, however. Camilla's energies, of course, were devoted to her music studies, although she also enjoyed literature, mostly Russian novels and English poetry. Ewald's time was taken up with both school work and his ongoing apprenticeship with his father, a widower now totally wedded to his work. Once, when Ewald lost his patience and threw a gouge chisel across the workshop, calling it useless, his father had given him another one of his stern lectures, saying, 'The art comes from a keen eye and a patient, steady hand.'

When summer returned, Camilla and Ewald resumed their love affair. One afternoon, while watching an Al Jolson comedy at the Maple Leaf Cinema, Ewald leaned over to Camilla and asked her to run away with him. 'We could go live in the country,' he whispered to her in the darkened movie house. 'I'd build you the most magnificent log cabin and we'd live on fresh air and the sweet sounds of your violin.' Ewald was a dreamer.

'Let's wait,' she told Ewald, squeezing his hand. 'We'll be together soon enough.'

Chapter 13

Camilla and Freda spent the afternoon sipping tea with Weller, whom they each found as charming as could be. Weller insisted that Freda play a song, and she obliged. My god, Freda thought, her heart thumping double-time, this might be the break I've been waiting for: a chance to play for a record producer.

Freda sat down at the piano and, taking a deep breath to settle her nerves, introduced the song.

'This is something I composed whilst living in Paris with my husband,' she said, looking over at Camilla for approval.

'Ex-husband,' Camilla whispered to Weller.

Freda, catching on, continued, 'He was a famous painter. Died of tuberculosis, I'm afraid.'

'Good!' Camilla commended.

Freda started the song, one of her best, a poignant ballad called 'Parachute' about setting a loved one free. But midway through the song, Freda stopped suddenly, her voice trailing off. She'd been looking at several framed photographs on top of the piano and suddenly noticed that the family depicted in each of them was black.

'Is there something wrong dear?' Camilla asked.

Freda got up, slowly. 'Mr Weller, is this your house?'

'No, of course not,' Weller replied. 'I abhor these Scottish baronial monstrosities.'

'Whose house is it?'

'Couldn't say,' said Weller.

'I think we'd better go, Camilla,' said Freda, putting down Camilla's teacup, grabbing her hand and leading her quickly out of the house.

As they hurried through a nearby field, with the sun quickly sinking behind the magnolia trees, Freda was bristling with rage. Camilla wasn't used to seeing Freda's temper, and was a little taken aback.

'You're not mad at me, are you, dear?' she asked, taking several fretful glances at Freda.

'No, I'm not mad at *you*. I'm mad at that, that *lunatic*.'

'He was not without a certain charm,' said Camilla.

'Camilla!' Freda stormed. 'He stole a car, broke into somebody's house and probably needed us for a satanic ritual. And on top of everything else, he pretended to be some famous, fucking high-and-mighty record producer.'

'Well,' said Camilla.

'Well what?'

'Well, isn't that what you wanted him to be, dear?'

Freda didn't respond. The sun had now gone down fully, it was already getting dark and a chilly breeze was picking up. 'Come on,' she said finally, 'we'd better get out of this wind or we're going to freeze to death.'

'I'm sorry, dear. The man *was* a rogue.'

'No, we no longer have rogues, Camilla. We have bloody psychopaths.'

Freda, of course, was mad with herself. She was mad that she'd allowed herself to be conned by Weller and that she'd played up to him. How incredibly naive of me, she thought. What if I hadn't spotted those photographs? Who knows how it could've wound up? She shuddered at the thought.

When they came to a crossroads on the highway, one sheltered by a stand of old oak trees, Freda announced that this would be as good a spot as any to start hitch-hiking. Immediately, she struck a pose with her thumb pointed in what she hoped was a northerly direction.

Camilla, noticing a highway phone booth kitty-corner to them, replied that this would be a good opportunity to try and reach Harold and tell him they were on their way to Toronto. As she set off to make her call, Freda worried about how long it would take for them to get a ride. Already, several cars had passed and it was getting darker by the minute.

Now it was Harold's turn to pace nervously about the police station. Why would anyone want to kidnap Ma, he thought to himself. Then he began to worry whether or not she'd been hurt.

'Isn't there something we should do?' he asked, somewhat frantically.

'We *are* doing something, Mr Cara,' said Kapur. 'We're waiting for that second phone call. Now, don't ask me why Mr Cara, but kidnappers always do this, okay? And more than this, I, personally, cannot do.'

Kapur excused himself and walked out of the police station, leaving Harold sputtering. Outside, he met Vince, who was standing on the dock. For an awkward moment, the two stood looking at each other. Vince offered a cigarette to Kapur, who politely declined. 'What do you think your wife's involvement in all this might be, Mr Lopez?' he asked.

'Oh, she masterminded it,' quipped Vince. 'She's a criminal genius.'

'Why the sarcasm, Mr Lopez?'

Vince decided to tell Kapur the truth, that he and Freda had had a big fight, that he'd been his usual dickhead self, as he put it, and that she'd stayed behind in Georgia.

'Now,' said Vince, 'I don't know if she's in Georgia or Toronto or somewhere in between.' Then, feeling really sorry for himself, he blurted out: 'I've lost my wife, Kapur.'

The kindly state trooper put his arm around Vince and the two walked back into the station. Harold, still pacing, looked up to see Vince with a cigarette in his mouth.

'At times like this, I wish I smoked,' said Harold.

'I know what you mean,' said Vince. 'When you're standing around like an asshole, it's nice to be able to smoke.'

Just then, the phone rang and Harold picked it up. It was his service calling with an urgent message.

'Yes? Uh-huh. This is he. All right, I'm ready,' said Harold, picking up a pencil. 'Uh-huh. Violin case. Okay. Forty-seven . . .'

Suddenly, Harold's tone changed abruptly. 'What? Oh, the Winter Garden in Toronto? What a surprise. Okay, okay. Oh, nice touch. Right.'

It was the kidnapper's second call. But this one had clearly got Harold's suspicions up. He was about to hang up when he remembered something. 'And the next time a Mr Rose calls,' he shouted into the receiver, 'ask if it's Jerry or Stanley!' And he slammed the phone down.

Vince and Kapur were standing, motionless, waiting for the explanation.

'Oh, this is real cloak-and-dagger stuff,' said Harold, shaking his head. 'We put forty-seven thousand dollars in a violin case,' he explained. 'Go to Toronto. Go to the Winter Garden Friday night. Check the fiddle. Hide the ticket in this particular statue – brother!'

With that, Harold stormed out of the station, muttering something about a nursing home.

Vince followed Harold out into the night air, caught up to him and asked what it was all about.

'Does she think I don't remember?' Harold roared. 'That statue, that fucking statue. Does she think I'm a total idiot?'

Vince was having difficulty following this. 'Does *who* think you're a total idiot?'

'Ma!' he screamed. 'My mother, of course. And then, as if that wasn't bad enough, forty-seven thousand – as if this is a number kidnappers pick out of thin air.'

Again, Vince was missing something. 'Forty-seven thousand?'

'Ma's got this thing about forty-seven thousand,' Harold explained. 'Years ago, I sold my parents' house in Toronto.'

'You sold the house?'

'Yeah, and ever since, she's got this thing that I owe her forty-seven thousand dollars.'

'You sold the house that you were raised in?' asked Vince, a bit incredulously.

'Don't look at me like that,' said Harold. 'She lives in a very nice house in one of the most agreeable and temperate climates in the world.'

Vince decided to ask about Freda. 'You think my wife's with her?'

'How should I know?' said Harold. 'That's your problem, keeping tabs on your wife.'

Seeing Vince turn, obviously hurt, Harold softened his tone. 'I've got my fucking hands full, Vince. My mother is not a well woman.'

'Gentlemen,' said Kapur, trying to calm both of them down, 'I suggest we all try to get a little sleep.'

Chapter 14

It wasn't long before Camilla's parents forbade their daughter from seeing Ewald. The turning point came when Camilla's mother found one of Ewald's love letters, a fairly florid piece of prose in which the boy had waxed rhapsodic about his feelings for Camilla, describing her hair as being like golden fleece and her lips the colour of rose petals. This was too much for Camilla's mother. Why wasn't he off playing hockey or football like normal boys, she wondered, instead of writing bad, Byronesque poetry to girls? Uncultured immigrants like him all grow up to be vulgar skirt-chasers, she thought, and she was having none of that for her daughter.

Ewald was devastated. His reactions, all wildly exaggerated as teenagers' emotions usually are, ranged from wanting to kidnap Camilla, to trying to reason with her parents. He even briefly considered killing himself. Finally, Ewald concluded that if he couldn't be with Camilla, he would simply leave the country. After consulting with his father, he decided on Austria, to study instrument-making. There, at least, he could throw himself into his craft, the way his father had done when Ewald's mother had died. Before he left, Ewald secretly met Camilla one final time and presented her with a new violin, an exquisite creation that would last her a lifetime. 'I'll treasure it always,' she told him.

Camilla did much the same, immersing herself in music while trying to forget about Ewald. Her lessons with Herr Professor Schoen were becoming increasingly demanding anyway, as he pushed Camilla to ever greater heights of advanced performance. The piece of music that they always reached for was, of course, the Brahms. But now their work on it involved all three sections, including the difficult, epic first movement and the fiery, gypsy-flavoured third. For Camilla, as for most violinists, the Brahms represented the ultimate challenge. And she promised herself that one day she would master it.

As time passed, Camilla grew up to become a beautiful young woman, refined but with a spunky independent streak. She learned her independence early on, when her parents took trips abroad, leaving Camilla alone in the care of a nanny. Although the family home in Rosedale, a wealthy midtown enclave, was large and spacious, she still yearned for the freedom she had enjoyed growing up, when her parents also owned a second property, a sprawling rural estate north of the city.

Shortly after her seventeenth birthday, Camilla's parents threw a large summer garden party, to which they invited many of their Rosedale friends and neighbours. Among the guests was an Italian couple and their son, who, before emigrating to Canada, had made their fortune with a wine vineyard near Napoli. The Caras were a cultured family, so Camilla's mother was happy to invite them.

When Camilla was first introduced to Ivor, she was immediately attracted to him. Although ten years her senior, Ivor was both dark and handsome. And the fact that he was also a writer added a certain panache to his profile, she thought. Once Ivor laid his eyes on Camilla, he turned on the charm and followed her about for the rest of the afternoon – much to the consternation of Camilla's mother, who watched them both very closely.

Within a week, Ivor had invited Camilla home for dinner. Despite her mother's strenuous objections, a courtship was well under way. When Ivor proposed, Camilla accepted, and her mother had little choice in the matter. The two were married in September and moved into a large, Victorian house that Camilla picked out in Cabbagetown, one of the oldest neighbourhoods in downtown Toronto. Ivor took one room for his study and told Camilla that she had the rest of the house to do with as she pleased. Quickly, she turned one of the extra bedrooms into a music room.

Chapter 15

A full day had passed since Camilla and Freda had first bravely stuck their thumbs into the wind. Now, twenty-four hours, five hundred miles and three long rides later – including an overnighter with a large, amiable trucker named Toots, the two women had arrived in Cincinnati, where they hoped to catch a train to Toronto.

The journey had been a little hard on Camilla. After sleeping up front in Toots' cabin, propped between him and Freda, she had awoken feeling not unlike a piece of luggage, stiff and somewhat rectangular. But she had made fast friends with Toots, having regaled him with a few of her extraordinary tales, including one about meeting the Earl of Farnsborough and discovering his fondness for shrimping, a kinky proclivity that involved sucking toes.

Freda, on the other hand, had only catnapped. Worried that Toots might nod off, she decided it was her duty to keep him awake by singing every road song she could think of, something she used to do with Vince whenever they took long car journeys. Freda sang Toots 'Twenty Four Hours from Tulsa' and 'Willin', the classic trucker's anthem. She even attempted 'By the Time I Get to Phoenix', although she secretly hated that one. And when she launched into 'Me and Bobby McGee', Toots surprised her by joining in. He especially liked the line about 'the windshield wipers slappin' time'.

Their last ride had been largely uneventful. A computer salesman, en route to Indianapolis, gave them an endless sermon about the information highway being 'the only true road to global peace', as he put it. Freda thought he sounded like a Moonie. Even Camilla couldn't get a word in edgewise. But at least he'd taken them as far as Cincinnati.

It was dark and rainy when they got out at the train station. Camilla bid the salesman adieu, while Freda smiled and waved, muttering 'good riddance' between her teeth like some sort of grouchy ventriloquist. As they entered the station, Camilla expressed the optimistic view that their train would likely be there and waiting. In fact, the station was all but empty. And the next train to Toronto wasn't until seven the next morning.

'We're in plenty of time, then,' said Camilla cheerfully.

Wandering over to some benches, they began assembling makeshift beds, folding old newspapers for pillows and using their jackets as blankets. Lying head-to-head with Camilla, Freda started to feel a dreadful *déja vu* coming on. 'This reminds me of the time Vince and I got bumped from our flight in Hawaii,' she said, staring up at the ceiling.

'Oh, enough of your outlandish stories,' scoffed Camilla. Of course, that didn't stop her from proceeding with one of her own. 'Did I ever tell you about my grand Russian tour?' she asked.

'Yeah, I think you did already,' replied Freda in a clearly disinterested tone.

'Russia! Oh yes,' said Camilla, now lost in her own world. 'I played St Petersburg. The conductor was the legendary Paderowski. He proposed to me after the performance. "But I'm married," said I. "Well then, sleep with me." "No, no, I couldn't." "Why not, if you say you love me? Do you love your husband?" "That's not the point. We are married. I have a son. What would become of him, little Harold?"'

Camilla dozed off eventually, leaving Freda awake and thinking about this woman and her endless calvalcade of tales. Camilla was a charming, spunky lady, Freda thought, but boy, could she go on. When Freda did fall asleep, it was only for a short while. She was awakened by a piece of music that piqued her senses. At first, she thought it was in her head, that the music, an ethereal melody played on a single violin, was merely part of a dream she was having. But then, as the melody dipped and soared and the violin's sound grew more resonant, she realized that it was something tangible right there in the room.

Sitting up, Freda looked across the station's marble floor. There, in a shaft of moonlight that streamed in through a long vertical window, Camilla stood, playing her instrument as effortlessly as someone breathing. For several, almost hallucinatory moments, Freda watched, transfixed, as Camilla made music as starkly beautiful as anything she had heard. As she listened, Freda felt an emotion – something from deep down inside – well up in her throat. It was as if this vision, this extraordinary woman whom she'd come to admire, represented at that moment everything she aspired to be yet could not become.

In a small town on the Georgia coast, Harold and Vince were having a Jack Daniels nightcap at the Overlander Motel, arguing about Kapur's competency and taking stock of their situation. Mostly, however, Harold was gnashing his teeth over his mother's scheme.

By the time he finished venting his spleen, Harold's tone softened and he began to use Vince as a sounding board to clear his nagging conscience.

'I think I'm making the right decision,' he said, trying to convince himself as much as Vince. 'Ma's being wilfully onerous.'

'I don't know *what* my wife's being,' said Vince, turning to his own dilemma. 'Do you think she's left me?'

A parallel conversation followed. 'The people from the nursing home can make the rendezvous,' continued Harold. 'I think it's the right decision.'

'My mother left my father,' said Vince, worrying about whether it was something in his genes. 'She just packed up and left. My dad didn't say one thing about it – just pretended like things were normal.'

'Ma never *left*,' said Harold, picking up a thread of continuity. 'But I thought she was going to a few times. One time, she even . . .' his voice trailed off. 'I guess my father wasn't the sort of man women leave.'

'Great guy, huh?' asked Vince, deciding it was time to throw the conversation over to Harold.

'Here's the kind of guy Ivor Cara was,' said Harold, warming to the tale. 'When I was a kid, I was a football fan, right? The Toronto Argonauts. I wanted to play for the Argos.' Vince looked at him in surprise. But there was a noticeable edge to Harold's voice. It was as if with this story of his childhood he was picking up the ball and running with it, albeit somewhat reluctantly.

'So I come home from school one day. Father says he has a surprise. We go out into the backyard and guess who's fucking-well there? Lionel Conacher!'

'Wow,' whispered Vince, at least recognizing the legendary sport figure's name.

'Harold the Lardbutt versus Lionel Conacher. He was only, what, athlete of the half-century or something? He could do it all, right? Football, lacrosse, baseball, boxing, wrestling, hockey, track and field. Anyway, he was the kind of guy who'd say things like, "Oh, looks like young Hal doesn't miss many meals." I hated that. So, anyway, we're running plays. After about the fifteenth time Lionel Conacher knocked me over, I just didn't bother getting up.'

Vince stared at Harold meaningfully. He was beginning to understand this guy with the double curse of having an overbearing father and being called Lardbutt in school.

'I think it's the right decision,' he said to Harold, finally, in a sudden show of compassion. 'The nursing home, I mean.'

Harold looked back at Vince, and decided to respond in kind. 'I don't think your wife has left you,' he told him. 'Now,' he said, standing, 'let's rack up some zeds.'

The idea of hitting the hay struck Vince as uncommonly sensible. He knocked back the last of his Jack Daniels, bid Harold sweet dreams and headed to his room.

That night, Harold tossed and turned. His dreams were anything but sweet. Rather, they were a troubling series of replays from his past adolescent fears, teenage traumas, adult humiliations. Worst of all, in one recurring nightmare, his father kept poking him repeatedly in the gut, demanding to know whether he had a 'bun in the oven'.

Vince, meanwhile, couldn't sleep. He'd been thinking about something Harold had told him earlier that day, and he'd come to a conclusion – one he wanted to confront Harold with right then. Jumping out of bed, he went down the corridor and kicked open Harold's door. Harold, clutching his covers to his chin, woke in a panic.

'You *do*, Harold,' hissed Vince, leaning in, just inches from Harold's face. 'You *do* owe your mother forty-seven thousand dollars.'

'Go back to bed, Vincent,' stammered Harold. 'This is personal family business.'

'Do you *have* forty-seven thousand dollars?' asked Vince.

'Yeah, yeah,' said Harold, 'but it's none of your . . .'

Before he could finish his sentence, Vince clamped one hand over Harold's mouth.

By the next afternoon, Camilla and Freda were halfway to Toronto. The train journey had given Freda a chance to close her eyes and ponder the choices facing her, and what her future might hold. For Camilla, it was an opportunity to drift back in time, back to a period in her life when her love for a young man rivalled the passion she felt for music. The romantic thoughts stirred her emotions; and once again, Camilla thought about what could have been.

Turning to Freda, suddenly, she said, 'I've decided that you *must* take a lover.'

Without opening her eyes, Freda quickly replied, 'It's enough trouble with just one man.'

But there was no stopping Camilla. 'You will emerge from the shadows naked,' she continued, 'modestly shielding yourself with pale, trembling hands.'

'Please,' said Freda, resisting the fantasy.

'What are you afraid of? Public scandal? They are peasants. Are you afraid of God? Do you think God wants you in this terrible union, this passionless existence?'

'Stop. All right?' Freda demanded, resenting Camilla's pushiness.

'Are you afraid of *him*?' asked Camilla. 'He won't hit you, he doesn't have to. His weapon is that he does not love you. He never has.'

Freda assumed Camilla was referring to Vince, although she was speaking with a strange conviction. Just then, the train lurched to a halt.

'This must be the border,' Freda said. 'Get your stuff ready.'

'You are such a meek little thing,' said Camilla, in a voice dripping with disgust.

'You don't know *what* I am!' said Freda, bristling with rage.

'I will tell you. You are what Ivor says you are!'

'Vince,' Freda corrected.

'Vince, Ivor,' shouted Camilla, 'what's the bloody difference?!'

'Look, I've had enough of this,' said Freda, who was just then stopped short by the appearance of a Canadian immigration officer. 'We were just having a little argument,' Freda told the official. 'You know how it is.'

'What's going on?' asked Camilla. 'Who is this man?'

The officer, a tall, lanky kid from southern Ontario's tobacco belt, carefully eyed the two women. 'I'll need to see some identification,' he said in his best deep, authoritative voice.

'Are we being arrested?' Camilla demanded to know. She was clearly flustered by this sudden intervention.

Freda handed over her driver's licence and birth certificate. Reaching into Camilla's carpet bag, she asked, 'This is where you keep your passport, isn't it, Camilla?'

'I've done nothing,' Camilla said indignantly. 'It's my money.'

Freda had no idea what Camilla was talking about, but she fished out an old yet pristine passport and handed it to the official, whose name-tag, she noticed, read: Drew MacPhail. To Freda's surprise, Camilla had a Canadian passport.

Officer MacPhail flipped through the passport; its pages were crisp with age and devoid of stamps or markings. When he turned to the photograph at the front, he saw it was that of a young woman. MacPhail's antenna went up straight away; this was awfully suspicious.

'This passport's expired,' he said pointedly. 'And it expired some years ago.'

Freda, who thought it strange that such a well-travelled woman should have such an unused passport, rushed to cover up on the expiry matter. 'I know what it is,' Freda said quickly, 'she grabbed the wrong one again. She's not very organized.'

MacPhail didn't buy it. He hadn't left his hometown of Tillsonburg and a likely future in tobacco farming for nothing. And he certainly wasn't about to be conned by two fast-talking women. 'Gather up your belongings, please,' he said, forcefully.

Freda grabbed Camilla's bag and began rifling through its contents. 'Come on, Camilla, you must have some other I.D. in here,' she said, eyeing MacPhail with unmasked disdain. 'Look,' Freda continued, 'she used to have a valid passport, so you know she's Canadian. Just because it's expired, it doesn't mean she's become a terrorist or something. Look, it says she was born in Toronto. I'm taking her there. It's important. Come on.'

This all sounded somewhat reasonable, but MacPhail decided to see how the old woman would respond to a border guard's first line of questioning. 'State the purpose of your visit, ma'am,' he asked briskly.

'The Brahms,' replied Camilla.

'The Brahms?' MacPhail queried. This was original, he thought.

'A violin concerto,' Freda explained.

'*The* violin concerto,' Camilla added. 'Almost impossible to play. I, um, *we* are going to attend a concert.'

'That's right,' said Freda, grateful for Camilla's more convincing display. 'A concert.'

MacPhail looked at the two women for another

moment. Too batty to be drug smugglers, he concluded, and then thrust the passport back at Camilla. 'You get that renewed in Toronto, ma'am, you hear?' As he walked away, MacPhail complimented himself on a fine display of discretionary judgement.

'Yes, all right, young man,' Camilla responded. As soon as he was out of earshot, she added, 'Although we're not going there straight away.'

This was news to Freda. 'What?' she asked in a loud whisper. Camilla just took Freda's hand and patted it, the way one would a small child's.

In the middle of the night, somewhere on a highway near the Ohio border, another confrontation was taking place. Vince was behind the wheel of Harold's rental car with Harold, in effect, his hostage. A heavy downpour was causing Vince to have to drive slowly and for the car's windshield wipers to go like the dickens. Harold, meanwhile, was peeved at Vince's impertinence. He had been squinting, trying to make out road signs, but the rainfall had made all but the numbers difficult to read. Finally, he caught the word 'Nashville' on a sign indicating an upcoming left-hand turn off the highway.

'I knew it,' said a bleary-eyed Harold. 'We're going to Toronto.' Oh boy, this kid Vince was something else, he thought. 'You want me to do this stupid money thing,' said Harold, now fully grasping Vince's plot. 'Only a seriously sick man would drive through this weather towards Canada.'

Vince ignored the comment. 'So why did your family move from Toronto, anyway,' he asked.

Harold yawned and rubbed his eyes. He desperately

needed sleep. 'My father liked the climate in Georgia,' he said, stifling another yawn. 'Thought it would be better for the flowers.'

Vince grappled with this revelation. 'You moved because of flowers?' he asked eventually.

Before he could get an answer, Harold was asleep and snoring. His snores were comical in the extreme, with a serious snort on the inhale and a ridiculous lip-fluttering on the exhale. It reminded Vince of Popeye. Then, looking down at Harold's considerable girth, he reconsidered: more like Popeye's fat foe, Bluto.

Vince drove through the night, stopping only for refills of gas and coffee. He searched the radio only to find country music from one end of the band to the other, an endless string of somebody-done-somebody-wrong songs. Not that he minded at first; the mournful laments seemed to suit his mood. By sunrise, however, he had started to notice an annoying pattern. Almost every song had mentioned either farms, prison, trains, trucks, mothers, dead dogs or Christmas. It made him think about Freda's songs, how they were blessedly free of such mundane clichés.

Just as he vowed to himself that he'd start appreciating Freda's music more, the car swerved wildly and began to shudder. 'Shit,' he said out loud, 'a flat.'

While Vince changed the tyre, Harold wandered down the highway and returned a short time later with a foot-long hot dog. Before finishing it, he contemplated the last morsel.

'Know what?' Harold asked, between chews, not waiting for Vince to respond. 'When you die, there'll be six pounds of undigested red meat in your system.'

Harold stuffed the last bite into his mouth with gusto.

'Hey, you know about those six ounces you supposedly lose when you die,' asked Vince, 'that some say is your soul?'

'Oh, sure,' said Harold, still masticating loudly.

'Is that true, or did your mother make that up?'

'Sure it's true,' Harold replied. 'Ma wouldn't make up something like that.'

Vince thought about this some more, as he finished changing the tyre.

Niagara Falls is the stuff of fables. The world's all-time, number one honeymoon spot. The setting of a classic Hitchcock-style thriller starring Marilyn Monroe. And the source of countless daredevil stunts – as well as one great Three Stooges gag.

To say that the Falls are breathtaking is to painfully state the obvious. As anyone who has taken a ride on the *Maid of the Mist* can tell you, there is simply no thrill to match the experience of being carried to the foot of the Falls and feeling the awesome power of three and a half million gallons thundering down one hundred and seventy feet around you. Charles Dickens, upon seeing them, opined: 'I seem to be lifted from the earth and to be looking into Heaven.'

Still, there is nothing heavenly about the small Canadian city that surrounds this natural wonder. The grease of one hundred fast-food outlets fills the air, competing with the noise of countless penny arcades for the attention of tourists – an estimated fourteen million a year. And it is said that the city's gaudy, neon-filled strip boasts more motels than any other street in the world. Now that's something to be proud of.

As Camilla took Freda past Tutankhamen's Tomb,

one of Niagara Falls' most popular attractions because it promised 'all the sights *and* smells from the Egyptian King's crypt', it occurred to Freda that this stopover was a senseless waste of time.

'Why exactly are we in Niagara Falls?' she asked, as they walked past a gaggle of giggling Shriners.

'Because I am a stupid old cow,' Camilla replied, almost bumping into two blond-haired boys and their ice-cream cones.

'Right. What else?'

'Never deny your heart,' Camilla told her. 'I'll tell you why, because everything else will pass, everything else will fade away, but your heart, your heart stays strong and young. If you deny your heart, it will destroy you.'

For a second, Freda wondered whether Camilla was answering her question or giving her advice. In the end, she decided that, at any rate, these were words worth remembering and thought that she should write them down in her notebook.

With twilight falling, they approached a wax museum. In the window stood a rogue's gallery of figures, movie stars, athletes and more than a few mass murderers, including Ted Bundy and Richard Speck. Freda shuddered as she passed these grisly characters. Camilla then led the way down an alleyway to a fire escape, which she began to climb. Just as Freda was about to demand where in the hell she was being taken, she heard some scratchy violin music at the top of the stairs. By the time Freda caught up with her, Camilla had knocked on a door and been greeted by a man with a grey goatee and a leather apron, who stood there staring at Camilla. Seconds, possibly minutes, passed.

'Well,' the man said at last. 'Son of a gun.'

This, of course, was Ewald. And he could scarcely believe his eyes. How long had it been? Forty, fifty years? He had dreamed many times about seeing Camilla again. Now that she was standing here before him, still a vision in white despite her advanced years, he wanted to soak up the image for as long as possible. But then he came to his senses.

'I'm forgetting my manners,' he said. 'Come in, come in.'

Camilla introduced Freda to Ewald, who took their coats and poured them each a glass of sherry. Sitting around his kitchen table, Ewald told Freda about his work as a violin maker. Freda, in turn, tried to describe to Ewald the kind of music she made, but was having as much trouble with that as she was in pronouncing his name.

'Ewald,' he told her, pronouncing it more or less as *ay-vault*.

'Ewald,' Freda enuniciated slowly.

'Sam,' Ewald said finally. 'Why not just make it Sam?'

'Hey, Sam,' said Freda. 'I know all about it. Freda – I'm named after my father's best friend, Fred Terkle. Now Camilla, there's a nice name.'

'Agnes,' groaned Camilla. 'My given name is Agnes.'

'I never knew that,' said Ewald.

'There are many things I never told you, Ewald,' said Camilla. 'If you had come to the concert as I'd asked . . .'

'Well . . .'

'. . . I would have left with you. I would have,' Camilla insisted, 'if you'd shown up.'

'I asked you to leave a thousand times,' countered Ewald. Camilla rose suddenly. 'Big day tomorrow,' she said, quickly changing the subject. 'Genius puts you in the tub, but only practice can get to those hard-to-reach places.'

'Again, please?' asked Ewald, shaking his head.

But Camilla had taken her exit, leaving Ewald and Freda alone at the table. For a few moments, there was a comfortable silence, during which they simply smiled at each other. Finally, Freda broke it with a question.

'Why *didn't* you go to the concert?' she inquired gently.

'I gave her many reasons to love me,' said Ewald, 'but nothing ever came of it. I thought that maybe if I gave her a reason to hate me we might both be free.'

In a funny sort of way, Freda understood the logic. 'Was she a great violinist?'

Ewald smiled a broad smile, accentuating all the creases in his face. 'The first time I saw her perform publicly,' he recalled, 'was in a church basement. A noon hour recital. Me and maybe three other people.'

As he talked, the two left the kitchen and walked into Ewald's workshop, half of which contained his workbench, littered with tools and wood shavings, the other half filled with antique display cabinets housing an assortment of Ewald's creations: violins, violas and cellos.

Ewald carried on with his reminiscence. 'Camilla comes on stage. She wears this ivory gown with a neckline that, well, it plunged. She began to play her violin. Played it like it was a hill and she was rolling down. With these beautiful breasts dancing along. Even now I can't think about it because I think my heart will stop.'

As Freda examined the instruments, including one double bass that she imagined someone like Harold would probably call a 'bull fiddle', she wondered whether Camilla and Ewald had ever consummated their love.

'But you and she never . . .?'

Ewald shook his head. 'After she moved away, I'd get letters, you know, about her travels. China. The Yukon. India. Then over the years I began to notice, it was always "I just got back from such and such." Not one postcard did I ever receive from "such and such".

Freda pondered this for a moment, remembering the passport without stamps, when she heard music coming from a room down the hall.

'Is this the Brahms?' she asked, trying to recognize it.

After a moment's consideration, Ewald shook his head. 'No, she's making this up as she goes along.'

They spoke for a while longer. But it was getting late, and, after showing Freda a couch in his workroom where she could bed down, Ewald said goodnight and went upstairs.

Shortly after Freda had drifted off, Camilla appeared, dressed in white, brocaded silk pyjamas. She peered at Freda, ensuring she was asleep, and then tiptoed up a short flight of stairs. Her heart was racing as she entered Ewald's bedroom. Ewald was not only awake, he was sitting up in bed, looking almost as if he was expecting a visit.

'I would have bathed in oils,' said Camilla, a little nervously, standing at the foot of Ewald's bed. 'I would have come dressed in a silken robe.'

Ewald smiled. 'I would have waited for you in

bed,' he answered, 'smoking black cigarettes from Bohemia.'

'I would stand by the foot of the bed,' said Camilla.

'I would stare, puffing away on the black cigarette from Bohemia.'

Camilla frowned. 'You never smoked, Ewald.'

'You never came to me wearing only a silken robe,' he grinned mischievously.

'I would have told you to turn down the lamp,' said Camilla.

'No.'

'Turn down the lamp,' Camilla gently urged. 'I'll slip off the silken robe and climb into bed.'

'The lamp stays on,' insisted Ewald. 'I want to look at you.'

'Very well. Can you see me now, Ewald?'

'I can. You are very *beautiful*,' he said, pronouncing the word with slow deliberation. 'They don't make bodies like that any more. That skin. It looks like it's never been touched by sunlight.'

'I suppose you think the breasts are a little on the small side,' said Camilla, self-consciously. 'Ivor does.'

'Ivor is an idiot,' said Ewald, with a note of anger.

'The nipples are so light they're almost invisible,' said Camilla apologetically. 'This is before I had Harold, mind you.'

'This is before any of it,' reassured Ewald.

'This is *before*. You should have come to the concert, Ewald. You should have come.'

'Yes,' Ewald agreed. 'I should have come.'

Camilla climbed into bed, and Ewald gently touched her face. That night, the two of them made love. It was sweet, gentle, yet passionate lovemaking unlike any Camilla had ever experienced. As she fell asleep with her head on Ewald's chest, she dreamed about dolphins dancing in the waves off the Georgia coast.

Chapter 16

Life with Ivor proved, rather quickly, to be one big unhappy charade. Camilla soon discovered that Ivor was a flirt, a dilettante and a philanderer. Though he fancied himself a serious novelist, he wrote cheap historical romances that barely concealed his own prurient interests. Once, when Camilla confronted him about the unmistakable female scent that permeated his body, Ivor claimed he'd been testing perfumes at a department store in search of one for her.

Ivor also developed a pronounced taste for liquor which, along with a hearty appetite for pasta, substantially added to his girth. His interest in Camilla seemed little more than an excuse to show her off to his drinking buddies who he'd bring home at all hours of the night. These were usually the only times that Ivor ever asked Camilla to play her violin. 'Mek some m-m-music fer our frens,' he'd slur drunkenly. 'Yes, dear,' she'd say, and proceed to play some innocuous piece of parlour music, whatever required the least passion on her part.

Camilla was growing restless. Her lessons with Herr Professor Schoen had come to an end. She had learned almost all that the Professor was able to teach her anyway. But she did miss performing; with marriage to Ivor, it had been pushed aside. And she thought that unless she could find some public forum for her music, she'd surely go mad. She decided to talk with Ivor. Perhaps she could begin giving a modest series of solo violin concerts in churches and school libraries around the city.

On the morning that Camilla was going to broach the matter with Ivor, however, she found that she was pregnant. Her doctor had called with the news, which left Camilla, initially, shattered. I'm not ready to have a baby, she thought. Then she asked herself, are Ivor and I even fit to become parents? She worried about this for several days, and refrained from telling Ivor the news. Finally, resigned to the fact that she was going to become a mother, she told Ivor, who was ecstatic. Camilla herself began to look positively on it, thinking that a baby might bring her and Ivor closer together, or that a family might at least provide the foundation that was clearly lacking in their relationship.

Harold proved to be a tubby little thing, taking after his father. Harold also proved to be a demanding child, and Camilla found that her plans to resume performing were put off. Finally, she convinced Ivor that she needed help with child care. After a few moments' thought, Ivor agreed. 'After all,' he said, 'I had a nanny and look how well I turned out.' Camilla simply bit her tongue.

Within a few years, Camilla had gotten back into her music, performing several times a month both as a solo artist and with several chamber groups. One day, while giving a noon-hour recital in a downtown church, Camilla was shocked to see Ewald in the audience. The sight of him flustered her greatly. But she played her violin for all it was worth. And she knew that she looked striking in her ivory gown with the plunging neckline. Afterwards, she and Ewald met for tea.

'You were breathtaking,' Ewald gushed.

'My playing, or my appearance?' Camilla asked.

'Both,' said Ewald, clasping her hand.

Chapter 17

The bus journey to Toronto passed without incident, despite the presence of a large group of Shriners. Freda figured out what had transpired the night before. She'd noticed the glow in Camilla's cheeks. And back at Ewald's, she'd overheard Camilla reciting a poem to him – the one she'd had trouble remembering on Fisherman's Island. It went: 'I must down to the seas again, to the vagrant gypsy life/To the gulls way, and the whale's way, where the wind's like a whetted knife/And all I ask is a merry yarn, from a laughing fellow-rover . . ./And quiet sleep and a sweet dream/when the long trick's over.' Freda then witnessed a touching scene, as Camilla leaned her head on Ewald's shoulder.

'I kind of thought maybe Ewald might have come to the concert,' Freda said eventually.

'Oh, no,' Camilla replied, shaking her head. 'He hates Brahms. If there's one thing Ewald can't stand, it's a German Romantic.'

As they went over Hamilton's Skyway Bridge, there wasn't a still fez on the bus. Shriners leaned and shifted to get a better view of Lake Ontario and Toronto's CN Tower, looming in the distance. A multitude of tasselled-coned hats bobbed at the windows, and Camilla, too, found herself looking at the lake. 'I remember once in Jariabad, the native girls stood naked by the edge of the water,' she said. 'They climbed on to the backs of dolphins and rode out to sea.'

Turning to Freda, she asked, 'Have you seen any whales, dear?'

'Yes,' said Freda, 'I saw a bull and a cow.' After pausing a moment, she added, 'They rose and sounded to each other, miles apart yet as close as they could be.'

'My goodness,' said Camilla. 'What an imagination you have.'

They arrived in Toronto late that afternoon and walked from the bus station to Freda's place, which was on a quiet residential street in the downtown. When they entered the Lopez apartment, Freda called out Vince's name. Hearing no reply, Freda offered Camilla a drink. 'I don't have any sherry,' she said, 'but I think I might have some Irish whiskey or maybe some vodka.'

'No dear, nothing,' said Camilla. 'Liquor clouds the mind.'

Freda checked messages on the answering machine, and caught her own pathetic confession: 'Hello, Vince? I did something stupid.' She quickly switched off the machine, hoping that Camilla hadn't heard it, and beckoned her down the hallway. 'Come on,' she said. 'I want to show you something.'

Leading Camilla into a room overlooking the street below, she said, 'This is where I make my music.'

The sun-drenched room was filled with instruments of every description: several guitars, including a National Steel, a banjo, a set of keyboards, some maracas and a trapezoidal-shaped thing called a dulcimer. Camilla cast her eye over the collection, stopping her gaze on the wall, which was covered in cork.

'That's so I don't disturb anybody,' Freda explained.

'It's a funny world where music disturbs people,' Camilla replied.

How true, Freda thought. 'Yeah,' she said, 'it's like once I saw a drunk singing on the subway. Everyone moved away, looked at him like he was dangerous or something.'

Camilla wasn't really listening. She was busy examining the contents of Freda's music room, including various pieces of futuristic electronic equipment, and had begun to look a little alarmed. 'Don't spend too much time in here, dear,' she told Freda. 'Promise me that.'

Although she didn't understand Camilla's concern, Freda nodded. 'Okay,' she said.

'Besides,' Camilla added, 'this isn't where you make your music. You make your music in your heart and your mind and with your lovely young fingers.'

As Camilla took Freda's hands and held them, Freda smiled and said, 'I better change.'

'Yes,' said Camilla. 'And put on something nice, dear. For the Brahms.'

A short time later, after both women had bathed and showered, Freda called to Camilla in the bathroom. 'Are you almost ready?' she asked, looking at her watch.

From behind the bathroom door, Freda heard Camilla

mutter: 'Buttons, buttons damned buttons. I'll be glad when they invent the zipper!'

Freda laughed. The bathroom door opened and Camilla stepped out, dramatically, dressed in a long ivory gown.

'Ooo-la-la!' Freda exclaimed. 'You're one beautiful woman, Agnes.' She meant it, too.

Toronto's Yonge Street is like a seedier, X-rated version of Niagara Falls' main drag. Equally garish, it too features an excess of neon signs, novelty shops and fast-food outlets. But added to that are dozens of stores that cater to the sex trade, with striptease, lap-dancing and the like.

Amid that cultural wasteland, from another era, sits the architectural jewel known as the Winter Garden. A grand old theatre, built at the turn of the century, it was originally a vaudeville house featuring performances by the likes of Milton Berle, Rose's Royal Midgets and the Shrapnel Dodgers, a troupe born in the trenches of World War I that featured one-eyed, one-armed and one-legged soldiers. Now, fully refurbished with real beech leaves, artificial blossoms and extravagant, hand-painted tree murals, it houses the finest in Broadway musicals and concerts, such as tonight's performance of the Brahms.

Harold and Vince arrived at the Winter Garden a good half-hour before show time. Harold, who had driven the last leg of the journey, pulled up in front of the theatre and stopped. Carrying a violin case, he got out and kicked the door shut, a tad violently.

'You're leaving the car here?' Vince asked, getting out of his side of the car.

'I'm not walking down Yonge Street with this thing full of money,' said Harold. 'Look at all these weirdos,' At that point, however, there weren't any panhandlers or rubbies on the street, only well-dressed concert goers. Harold stepped up to the booth, purchased two tickets and he and Vince entered the theatre. As he nervously exchanged the violin case for a tag at the coat check, he told the young woman, 'Take very good care of this, please.' Then he led Vince through the foyer.

'Come on,' Harold said, heading out into the Winter Garden's courtyard. 'I know what statue she means. My mother used to bring me here.'

'To hear concerts?' asked Vince.

'No, so she could meet a man.'

'Really?'

'No, I lied,' said Harold. 'Of course, really, putz. And she'd make me sit underneath this statue and wait for her,' he added, pointing to a large angelic stone figure. 'She said I was safe with the angel. And so I'd sit there and watch.'

As he said this, Harold unconsciously sat down at the foot of the angel and continued his story. 'This man would pull up in a big black Packard. Remember those? Excellent cars. Well crafted. I wish I had one of those babies. They last forever. Even Cadillacs aren't what they used to be.'

Vince had to steer Harold back to his story. 'So, this man pulled up in a black Packard . . .'

'Right,' said Harold. 'And I'd watch. From right here. This is her,' he added. Getting up, he touched the stone angel's face. 'She's so much smaller than I remember. I even had a name for her, Elizabeth.'

Harold felt himself getting anxious, so he sat down. 'One time,' he said, trying to keep his composure, 'one time Ma almost got into the car and drove off with the guy. I know that. I sat here and watched. She had one foot in the car, the other on the sidewalk. She looked back at me and the angel.'

Swallowing hard, Harold continued. 'I yelled. Boy, I hollered. "Don't get in the car, ma. Don't get in the car."'

Harold fell silent for a moment. He stood up slowly and tucked the coat-check tag in the crook of the angel's arm. He turned to Vince. 'They got a bar in there, you figure?'

'Sure,' said Vince, visibly touched at Harold's story, 'I think I saw a bar.'

'C'mon, I'll buy you a drink,' said Harold, putting his arm around Vince's shoulders.

While Vince and Harold were imbibing in the Winter Garden's upstairs lounge, Camilla and Freda arrived at the theatre. Camilla had brought her violin, which she took to the coat-check, telling the young woman behind the counter to take 'very good care of this'. As she handed it over, she added, 'It's my violin.' The coat-check raised her eyebrows, as if to say, Oh, is *that* what it is. Camilla stuffed the tag inside one of her evening gloves and, since there were still a few minutes before the concert, she told Freda she wanted to show her the courtyard and took her outside.

It was a balmy evening, and the courtyard, illuminated by lamposts and white fairy lights on the trees which lined the walkway, was quiet. Camilla began to tell the whole story of her performance at the Winter Garden many years before.

'All of Toronto High Society was here,' she told Freda, who smiled and looked about the courtyard, trying to imagine the times. 'They arrived in carriages, you know, people didn't use automobiles back then, not to attend an event like this.

'Snow was falling. It lightly tumbled down. It danced.' As she spoke, Camilla stepped up to the large stone angel and extracted the hidden coat-check tag and clenched it in her first.

'The people came to see Camilla Cara,' she continued. 'I wore this ivory dress, dear. The neckline plunged. Ivor was furious – said he wouldn't allow it. I told him, if I don't wear this dress, I wear nothing. And I would have done it – I would have walked out naked.'

Freda laughed at Camilla's boldness. But something had changed in the older woman, and her voice dropped in volume a little as she carried on with the tale. 'There was silence as I took to the stage. I drew out the first note,' said Camilla. She stopped abruptly.

'Do you know, dear, I hadn't rosined my bow correctly. The first note . . . well, there was a little squeal. Somebody laughed. Somebody *laughed*. I could see him sitting right in the front row, a fat man. A friend of Ivor's. He laughed.'

Freda could see the trauma in Camilla's face. 'You didn't care,' Freda told her, 'they're all peasants.'

'Brahms must have been a very vicious man, to write such a piece full of little traps,' Camilla continued. 'The hardest passage, the very hardest part, I played well.

Then, I was so relieved that I'd done it, the next bar I got confused. I made a mistake. I lost my place.'

Camilla was beginning to cry. 'Maybe no one noticed,' offered Freda, assuringly.

'Why do you keep saying no one noticed?' asked Camilla, almost angrily. 'Everybody noticed. The fat man kept laughing. And soon, more people were laughing. Ivor was blushing. He was *ashamed* of me. I was never ashamed of him, even when he wrote books that were junk and piffle. The audience started laughing. Some booed, others jeered. And I thought, *never* . . .'

As Camilla turned abruptly away, crying with her head in her hands, Freda finished her sentence. 'Never again.'

'I'm sorry, dear,' said Camilla.

'Sorry?' replied Freda. 'For what? What you did, what you didn't do, that doesn't matter. That's not important. What's important is . . . you kept yourself, you know, your *self*, going. And here you are, and I think you're fucking amazing.'

'It wasn't all lies,' said Camilla, smiling and starting to regain her composure. 'I have done some travelling. I've seen that place where God has split the world in twain.'

'The Grand Canyon?' asked Freda.

'That's it,' Camilla replied.

As the sound of the orchestra tuning up drifted out into the courtyard, the two women started walking back. 'Let's go hear if this Tinscheff person can get any blood pumping through the Brahms,' said Camilla. Then she added, 'I *can* play the silly thing, you know.'

'I know you can,' said Freda.

'Just not if anybody's listening.'

Chapter 18

It was a surprisingly unselfish move – even for Ivor. One night during the winter of 1927, from out of the blue, Ivor announced to Camilla that he'd booked the Winter Garden for May first so that she could hold her own concert. He'd even hired the string section of the Toronto Symphony to accompany her and ensured that the concert would be well promoted. When she had recovered from the shock, Camilla decided it was the perfect occasion for her to give her public debut of the Brahms.

On the night of the concert, Camilla could barely sit still. She knew the music backwards, of course, and had rehearsed twice with the symphony string section, but she was terrified at the prospect of the performance. And she didn't feel she could admit any of this to Ivor, who had invited all of his friends and told her that he hoped she wouldn't let him down in front of them.

As Camilla stood in the wings of the Winter Garden's stage, nervously clutching her violin, her thoughts turned to the instrument's maker. Ewald had lovingly constructed it the year that he'd left for Austria, before Camilla's parents forbade her from seeing him again. Camilla had grown up with that instrument, hearing its sound mellow and become more full-bodied over time, the way a wine's taste does with age. When Camilla had told Ewald of her news about the concert, he was thrilled that she was going to play the Brahms in public on the violin he'd made specially for her.

She had told Ewald that she wanted him to come to the concert. And Ewald, sensing one last opportunity, gave her a conditional agreement. 'I'll come to the concert,' he had said, 'if you run away with me.'

'I'll think about it,' Camilla had replied.

As she waited to go on, Camilla wondered where Ewald might be sitting, and she found the thought of him being somewhere in the audience reassuring. Then, as she began to rosin her bow, a burst of clarity came over her: I *will* run away with Ewald tonight, she decided. But first, I must get through this performance.

When she stepped out, the sound of applause carried her all the way to centrestage. Dressed in her ivory gown, Ewald's favourite, she stood, motionless, with the violin tucked under her chin. As the orchestral exposition of the first movement drew to a close, Camilla lifted her bow and began to play the opening flourish of notes, the fast ascending and descending ones that establish the violin's presence in the work. She closed her eyes and gave herself over to the Brahms.

But as the notes rang out into the auditorium, Camilla realized there was something terribly wrong. The sound was harsh, not crisp, and she cringed when the violin suddenly emitted a squeal. Camilla was sure everyone had heard it as well, which jangled her nerves badly. But she kept on playing. Then midway through her part, just as she was required to play a series of fast arpeggios, Camilla became distracted and lost her place. What was worse, she started on a passage and then stopped, realizing that she'd jumped her cue.

This last gaffe, the audience *had* noticed. One of Ivor's cronies, a portly, inebriated man in the third row, who was there only to please his wife, actually let out a laugh. This signalled Ivor's other buddies, who began snickering loudly. Before the laughter dissolved into outright boos and jeers, Camilla burst into tears and fled from the stage. She ran to the courtyard, desperately hoping to find Ewald there, waiting to take her away. But he never showed up.

Chapter 19

Up in the Winter Garden's bar, Harold and Vince were killing time. Harold, visibly agitated, was making small talk, flitting from subject to subject like a butterfly in springtime, never alighting long enough for Vince to catch his drift.

'. . . they wilt, you know,' said Harold, in mid-non-sequitur, 'and this seems somehow contrary to, well, I'm agnostic, but even so I'm tempted to say, contrary to some grand design . . .'

Vince cut him short. 'Don't take this the wrong way, okay,' he said, 'but you're just blithering away like an idiot here. When you started off, it had something to do with flowers.'

Harold, a little startled by Vince's sudden confrontation, responded in a similar fashion. 'Okay,' said Harold, 'from where I stand, you keep Freda locked away.'

'That's horseshit,' said Vince indignantly. 'I don't

keep her locked away. She can do what she likes.'

'And you're sneaky like my dad was,' Harold continued. 'You'd never say, "Don't do it," you only say, "It's just a stupid little hobby." Right?'

Vince didn't respond. He and Harold watched the last of the patrons head through the doors to their seats. For an awkward few moments, they simply stared at each other.

'I'm not much of a classical music fan,' Vince finally confessed.

'It's the Brahms,' said Harold. 'Me, I can take it or leave it.'

Camilla and Freda took their seats in the auditorium's balcony. As they settled in, the two gazed about at the Winter Garden's decor, resplendent in shades of leafy green. The orchestra was tuning up, and the auditorium was abuzz with the usual pre-concert chatter. But it quickly fell silent when Lauron Tinscheff, dressed in a black, sleeveless gown, stepped out on to the stage. Young and blonde, she was quite beautiful, thought Freda, who was studying her every move, her focus, her concentration, as the violinist readied herself to play.

Camilla turned to Freda, excitedly, and smiled. Freda took the old woman's hand and gave it a squeeze. While the orchestra started in on the first movement, they watched as Tinscheff stood with her eyes closed. Then, raising her violin to her chin, Tinscheff began playing her introductory solo. Camilla leaned to Freda and whispered, 'Here comes the tricky part.'

The young violinist pulled it off brilliantly, managing the solo's difficult ascending notes as deftly as she did the fluid descent into a rhapsodic middle section. Camilla closed her eyes, reliving her own love affair with the music. Smiling approvingly, she even applauded at one point, although more to herself than at any audible level.

Freda, too, had become seduced by the inspiring sight of a young woman mastering a complex piece of music with such confidence. If only Vince could see this spectacle, she thought, maybe he'd understand why music is so important to me. But just as Freda was giving herself over to the epic sweep of the first movement – which she now remembered first hearing on the radio during the drive down to Georgia with Vince – Camilla turned to her, pressed a coat-check tag gently into her hand, stood up and said, 'Goodbye, dear.'

Camilla rushed to the exit door of the auditorium. But as she pushed it open, she froze, having caught sight, she thought, of a small, chubby boy standing, expectantly, in the lobby. He looked so much like the young Harold. Racked with fear and guilt, she stood, unable to move. After a few minutes, Freda arrived to find Camilla petrified and helpless. Pushing the door ajar, Freda saw Harold standing there with his hands in his pockets. Studying the old woman's stricken face, she said, 'Camilla, it's a Texas gate. It's only a Texas gate.'

'But I can't,' said Camilla.

Freda took one more long look at Camilla and then stepped through the door herself. There, she greeted both Harold and Vince.

'Freda!' Vince exclaimed, totally surprised to see her.

'Where's my mother?' asked Harold frantically.

'Oh, she's in the washroom,' Freda replied, quickly

leading both men across the lobby to a staircase.

'What washroom?' Harold demanded.

'She's been in there twenty minutes, or something,' said Freda. 'I'm kind of worried about her.'

'Twenty minutes!' shouted Harold. 'Why didn't you . . . she never goes to the washroom by herself.'

'Come on,' said Freda, 'I'm going there now.'

As the three started up the staircase, Camilla made her getaway, picking up a violin case at the coat-check before rushing for the rear doors.

Just then, Harold noticed a washroom sign pointing in the other direction. 'Wait a minute,' he said, 'the washroom's down this way.' As he turned, he spotted his mother in full flight. 'Ma!' he screamed.

Camilla ran for all she was worth, with Harold in hot pursuit. As Freda and Vince rushed to catch up, Harold summoned a security guard who was sitting nearby. 'Stop that old lady!' he shouted. The security guard, who dropped a cup of take-out coffee in the commotion, gave chase.

'Run, Camilla,' Freda screamed.

Vince raced after them, took a leap and caught the security guard with a flying tackle just as he neared Camilla. While the men grappled on the floor, Camilla was able to slip out through the doors. Harold and Freda followed her out.

'Ma!' screamed Harold. Camilla had run through the courtyard and reached the kerb, where a large black Packard, in immaculate condition, stood waiting. Camilla opened the passenger door and, with one foot in the car, turned to look back at Harold who'd stopped running.

After a long moment's silence, Harold swallowed

hard and yelled, 'Get into the car, ma! Get into the car!' It was as if, with those simple words, Harold had freed both his mother and himself from the longstanding chains of dependency.

Camilla smiled a radiant smile and climbed into the Packard, gleaming in the light of the theatre's marquee. Harold, Freda, Vince and the roughed-up security guard stood and watched as the car pulled away.

Inside the car, Camilla tried to catch her breath. She didn't know whether to laugh or to cry. Ewald, behind the wheel and dressed in a white tuxedo with a ruby-red bowtie, simply beamed at her. 'Sorry I was a little late,' he told her. 'There was such a lot of traffic – imagine.'

'Oh, my goodness,' said Camilla, clutching her violin case excitedly. 'My heart is beating so quickly.'

'That's a good sign,' Ewald deadpanned.

'Oh, my goodness,' Camilla said again.

Ewald pulled the Packard over and stopped. Reaching behind Camilla's seat, he picked up a new violin case. 'Here,' he said, 'is a present for you.'

Camilla opened it and picked out the most magnificent instrument she'd ever seen. She gasped at its beauty and fondled its smooth contours before cradling it in her lap. She could not have dreamed of a more fitting gift.

'Well,' she said expectantly, 'what are you waiting for?'

Ewald, quoting from their favourite poem, replied, '"A quiet sleep and a sweet dream, when the long trick's over."'

As Camilla smiled, Ewald leaned over and gently kissed her. Camilla returned it, lovingly. It was one of those kisses, long and meaningful, that seemed to last an eternity.

Chapter 20

In the Winter Garden's courtyard, Freda finally opened her hand to discover the coat-check tag that Camilla had slipped her inside the auditorium. She called after Harold and gave him the ticket. Without a moment's hestitation, Harold plucked it from her and headed back inside the theatre. Vince, standing there alongside Freda, was feeling awkward. As he watched Harold leave, he attempted to break the ice.

'He's a nice guy,' Vince ventured.

'Harold?' said Freda, dubiously. 'You think?'

'People don't understand Harold.'

'And you do?' she said, moving towards a bench.

'Yeah, I do,' said Vince. 'He's afraid.'

'Afraid of what?' asked Freda.

'The same thing everyone else is afraid of, I guess.'

'What are you afraid of?'

Vince took a deep breath. 'I'm afraid that you may get up one day, play your music, and it might not go well and it'll hurt. And at the same time, I'm afraid it will go well and I'll lose you to your music.'

Freda looked at Vince, and was moved at this rare display of vulnerability. She sat down. 'I don't understand why it has to be like that,' she said.

'It doesn't,' said Vince, sitting down next to her. 'It doesn't, Freda. Look, this is my best shot, Freed. You got six ounces, right, I got six ounces. Put them together – bingo – you got a pound.'

'There's not twelve ounces in a pound,' said Freda. 'There's sixteen.'

'We're talking about our life together,' said Vince, getting a little exasperated. 'I don't think we should get all tripped up over whether there's twelve or sixteen ounces in a pound.'

Harold interrupted, carrying a violin case. 'Sixteen,' he said. 'Except if you're measuring precious metals or gems or something like that. Then it's only twelve.' With that smug little display of his knowledge of weights and measurements, Harold handed the violin case to Freda.

'Here,' said Harold, 'you keep that.' Then he added, 'I guess Ma wanted you to have that.'

As he turned to go, Vince called after him, 'Don't you want to know what's in it?'

'No,' said Harold, walking away. 'If it's the fiddle – I mean, the violin – that's nice. If it's the money, I don't want to know about it.'

Money? Freda was confused.

'Harold!' yelled Vince.

'Yeah?'

'We'll talk.'

'Okay,' said Harold, as he went back inside the theatre.

Freda opened the violin case. There inside was Camilla's precious violin. She closed the case and, in a gesture not unlike what Camilla would've done, clasped it to her chest. Then Vince finally spoke.

'You know your song, Freed, that beautiful song that you wrote?' He started to recite the lyrics to 'Parachute'. '"If I could give you anything . . ."' but he couldn't remember how it finished. 'How does it go, Freed?'

'". . . I'd give you back your self."'

'That's right,' said Vince. 'I would. I will.'

'Okay,' said Freda, smiling as she stood up. She put her arms around Vince and they kissed longer and more passionately than they had in a long time.

Finally, Freda pulled away and said, 'So, what are we going to do now?'

'We could go on vacation,' said Vince.

'In what?' asked Freda. And they both burst out laughing.

Chapter 21

The following week, Freda and Vince were back in Peabo, Georgia. They spent their afternoons mostly making love – and music, with Freda singing her songs and Vince dancing around the cottage sometimes wearing nothing but a towel. Many nights, Freda could be found at the Fishin' Hole, where she'd become a popular fixture, capable of silencing even the most diehard hecklers.

As for the Brahms, Freda never did hear all of it that night at the Winter Garden. But the music stayed with her for many years to come. She heard it in the gift of the violin that went with her everywhere. And sometimes, at sunset, she could swear she heard its melody travelling across the sea.

Not across the sea, but somewhere up the coast, an elderly couple stood barefoot on a beach, watching the sun dissolve into the horizon. Camilla was playing her violin, casting notes out on to the water, as if to some aquatic audience down below. Ewald listened to the music, which drifted back to shore like waves gently lapping at his feet. And when Camilla finished the piece, an improvised number that she played from the heart, Ewald applauded proudly. Taking a long, gracious bow, Camilla smiled and silently thanked the sea for its magic.